The Bongleweed

When he came up to hand over the half-empty envelopes, she found herself smiling at him for the first time, happy in the thought that he had sown his own doom with his own hands.

'I wasn't too sure what this one was.' He was holding out the airmail envelope. Her heart jumped a beat. 'But I sowed it anyway. There weren't many, and I've used them all, I'm afraid. What is it?'

'Oh, that,' she heard herself saying carelessly. 'Probably the South American Bongleweed.'

Helen Cresswell was born in Nottingham and graduated in English Honours from King's College, London. *The Piemakers* was first in a distinguished series of fantasies that includes *The Nightwatchmen*, *The Bongleweed*, and *Up the Pier*, all nominated for the Carnegie Medal. She is also noted for the wickedly humorous *Bagthorpe Saga* and is a leading writer of children's television drama, twice BAFTA nominated. Series include original drama, *Lizzie Dripping* and *Moondial*, and adaptations include E. Nesbit's *The Phoenix and the Carpet* and *The Demon Headmaster* by Gillian Cross. She lives and works in a small Nottinghamshire village.

The Bongleweed

Other Oxford stories you might enjoy:

The Bongleweed

Helen Cresswell

Illustrated by Tim Archbold

OXFORD
UNIVERSITY PRESS

OXFORD
UNIVERSITY PRESS

Great Clarendon Street, Oxford OX2 6DP

Oxford University Press is a department of the University of Oxford.
It furthers the University's objective of excellence in research, scholarship,
and education by publishing worldwide in

Oxford New York

Athens Auckland Bangkok Bogotá Buenos Aires Calcutta
Cape Town Chennai Dar es Salaam Delhi Florence Hong Kong Istanbul
Karachi Kuala Lumpur Madrid Melbourne Mexico City Mumbai
Nairobi Paris São Paulo Singapore Taipei Tokyo Toronto Warsaw

with associated companies in Berlin Ibadan

Oxford is a registered trade mark of Oxford University Press
in the UK and in certain other countries

First published by Faber & Faber 1973

Oxford edition published 1999
Reprinted 1999

British Library Cataloguing in Publication Data available

Cover illustration by Tim Archbold

ISBN 0 19 275032 1

1 3 5 7 9 10 8 6 4 2

Typeset by AFS Image Setters Ltd, Glasgow

Printed in Great Britain
by Cox & Wyman Ltd, Reading, Berkshire

*To Olive and Richard Kennedy
with love*

Whatever a man prays for, he prays for a miracle. Every prayer reduces itself to this: 'Great God, grant that twice two be not four.'

Ivan Turgeniev

Chapter One

'Oh, *Dad*,' said Becky. 'Polishing spades *again*!'

'A good workman,' he began, not even lifting his head.

'Oh, I know,' she said quickly. 'Don't tell me again. I believe you.'

She turned a grass-box endways on and sat down because whatever she might say, she loved the potting sheds and outhouses, with their smells of lime and creosote and whitewash and oil and old grass shavings. They were smells she had grown up with and meant home to her, really, even more than those of their own house.

'When's this boy coming?' she asked. 'He'll be no good, you'll see. Sounds like some sort of *weed*, or something. You should've heard Mrs H. going on to Mum about him. "Such a delicate boy, Elsie, and so highly strung. His mother says he's outgrowing his own strength." I ask you! How on earth can you outgrow your own strength? Either you've got no strength, and you stop a pygmy, or you've *got* strength, and you grow. Obvious.

What's he supposed to have had? Yellow jaundice? It didn't kill *me*. Nothing to it.'

'Let him alone till you've seen him,' said Finch, ranging his spades methodically according to size along the wall—like a family in order of age, thought Becky, or the Three Bears except that there were five of them.

'I can hardly wait,' she went on. 'He'll be all long and pale, like forced rhubarb.'

'That he might be,' replied Finch. 'But he's got brains, and that's something in his favour. Wins scholarships.'

'Well he'd be bound to, wouldn't he?' said Becky. 'Being a *Harper*.'

Finch turned and looked at her, straddling the grassbox and rocking it dangerously from side to side. The look was reproving and familiar.

'You're quick enough on the uptake yourself, Becky, if you'd steady up a bit. But you've no respect for things that matter.'

'Oh, *Dad*!' She stood up, her legs sticking momentarily to the warm metal. She opened her mouth to say something else, then changed her mind, and closed it. She knew by now that it was no good arguing with him about that, or about the Harpers. To him they were perfect—the pivot of his existence. The doctor in particular. The doctor, she reflected, might as well be *God*, the way her father worshipped him. Guiltily she checked the thought—the cool, faintly musty potting-shed smell reminded her somehow of the inside of a church.

'I didn't *mean* it,' she whispered to herself, just to put things right.

Finch, who always took off his cap when he came indoors, just as if he *were* in church, picked it up now from the nail by the door and levelled it squarely above his ears.

'He's coming today,' he told her. 'I'm to drive down and fetch him, four fifteen.'

'Can I come?'

She already knew the answer.

'It wouldn't do. I'm taking the doctor's car.'

'We wouldn't want his poor thin little bones to be rattled round in our old banger, would we?' she said sweetly, taking a swipe at a cobweb and watching a startled spider whirl out at the end of a long thread.

'I hope, Becky,' came his voice over his shoulder, 'that you'll find you can get on with the lad. It'll be an opportunity for you, having a lad like that here for a month or two, and I hope you'll make the most of it.'

She followed him out, blinking in the strong early morning sunlight.

'Oh, *Dad*,' she said. 'You're so old-*fashioned*.'

'I'm neither old nor new nor anything else fashioned,' came back his obstinate voice. 'I'm Albert Finch, and I know what I think.'

'Well, I'm Becky Finch, and I know what *I* think,' she said rebelliously to herself. Then, aloud:

'Where're you going now, Dad? The Jungle House?'

He nodded. A good deal of his conversation was normally carried on by nods and shakes. It was almost like a kind of morse code to people who knew him. It was easy to see why he wore his cap so square-on. At any other angle, it would scarcely have survived a bare two minutes' conversation.

They walked single file along the paved path that followed the dividing wall between the working gardens and the gardens proper—Pew Gardens. The same weathered brick wall divided their own end of the long, rambling house from the main part where Dr and Mrs Harper lived. Finch opened the arched wrought-iron gate and Becky followed.

As she looked beyond her father's broad-shouldered back to the scene beyond, a little sigh of pure pleasure escaped her lips. It was no use, she simply could not help herself. Because the sight of the smooth lawns, and beyond them the budding trees where the hexagonal glass tropical house swam and shimmered in a pale green mist, was beautiful.

'Where else in the world,' she asked herself for the thousandth time, 'is anywhere *near* so green?'

Despite her impatience with Finch and his everlasting green fingers and slow, unswerving patience, she loved Pew Gardens with a fierce, possessive love that she admitted to no one, not even herself. She loved especially the early morning hours, summer and winter alike, when the Gardens were theirs alone, a secret and inviolable world where the traffic beyond the distant walls was a mere muffled reminder that any other kind of world at all existed behind them. When the gates opened to the public at ten and the first visitors passed through the turnstiles, she would turn her back on it, returning only sometimes at sunset to gloat over the restored silence, and pick up the odd dropped paper bag or ice-cream carton.

'Savages!' she would mutter under her breath, unconsciously mimicking the doctor. 'Heathens! Lousy little littermongers!'—the last being a phrase of her own invention whose alliterative flourish gave her particular pleasure.

She walked with long strides, fitting her own feet into the prints left in the dewy grass by her father's boots. She was so deep in the exercise that it was with something like shock that she found herself all at once on gravel. Finch delved for his bunch of keys and unlocked the door of the glasshouse with the usual grave ceremony.

Next minute she was breathing the hot, steamy air, suffocating after the thin dawn coolness outside. Here the green came crowding in with a rush, a green so brilliant and surging that sometimes when she was alone Becky would think that if she stood long enough she would actually *see* things growing. In here there was always the sound of water, trickling, splashing, and mesmerizing, till by the time you were barely a few steps into the undergrowth it seemed actually possible that you were in a real jungle.

Usually her father took his time on his first visit of the day, stopping here to tie back a stray tendril, there to test the rubberiness of a stem. This morning he walked steadily forward with hardly a glance about him.

'What have you come to look at, Dad?' asked Becky. 'Is it the cross?'

She looked up and saw the uncapped head nod briefly.

'One of these days,' she remarked, 'he'll go and *really* get something crossed up.'

'The doctor is a *scientist*, Becky,' came her father's voice, oddly blurred and altered by the thick wet atmosphere.

'Even a scientist must leave some things to chance,' she said. 'He doesn't know *everything*, does he? And why's he always got to be *crossing* things? Aren't there enough different plants and things in the world already, without his inventing new ones?'

She nearly added 'As if he were God, or something,' but remembered her earlier discomfiture, and refrained.

'Science,' said Finch, 'ain't one for standing still. The doctor's experiments'll likely change the whole course of civilization.'

Here we go, she thought. A Potted Harper Lecture.

'All right, Dad,' she said hastily. 'How's it going, anyhow? Is that it? *That?*'

She pointed to a row of tall thick-stemmed plants enclosed within a separate cloche among several like it on a sort of built-up island in the very centre of the glasshouse.

'It's grown, hasn't it?'

She looked sideways and saw that his face was a deep, suffused pink. He pulled a metal measure from his pocket and leaning forward carefully removed the cloche and put it down to one side.

'But, Dad, you only put them in two days ago.'

He was nodding, and his square-tipped fingers shook slightly as he stretched out the silvery measure

against the tallest of the plants. As she watched,
he stopped nodding and began to shake his head
instead, staring down at the number his thumb
had marked before pushing the reel back into its
case again. Becky, watching, read the signs.

'It's something good, isn't it, Dad? The doc's
really done something at last!'

Still he did not reply. He had pocketed the
measure and was now tapping the bulge it made in
his pocket and shaking his head at the same time.

'*What*'s he done?' she cried.

Again he shook his head.

'Oh, *Dad*!'

Exasperated, she craned forward and peered

herself at the seedlings. It seemed queer to think of them as seedlings at all, nearly two feet high as they were, and bushing thickly at the base of their stems. But she knew for a fact that they had been planted only on Monday, and today was Wednesday. So seedlings they were, she supposed, but freaks, as if a new baby had shot ten feet high after its first few bottles.

Her father was clearing his throat and she looked enquiringly at him.

'They're making very good growth,' he admitted at last. 'Very good indeed.'

He lifted the cloche and replaced it gently. Becky shrugged. 'Oh, if that's all . . .' she said.

He gave the plants a final, thoughtful stare, and then began to walk on in a manner that Becky recognized. He was starting now on his rounds proper.

'I'm off, Dad!' she called after him. He nodded.

Outside, she paused for a moment to take in several long gulps of the cool air before setting back towards the house. She would have to get her own breakfast, and her father's, too, she knew for a fact. Her mother, who 'did' for the Harpers, would be round there already, getting *their* breakfasts.

Its a fine life, she thought, for the rich . . .

Chapter Two

Becky let herself in at the back door and saw that everything had been left ready. Half-heartedly she shook out a bowl of cornflakes and sat down. Almost immediately she got up again and went through into the narrow passage and across it into the little beamed parlour. Not that it was really a parlour—it couldn't be—no one had a parlour these days. But that was what *they* called it, though she herself called it the 'lounge' whenever her friends from the new houses in the village came round. She crossed to the far wall, which had been built when the house had been divided into two parts.

Just before last Christmas, Mrs Harper had taken it into her head that she wanted a recess in her side of the wall, for ornaments and books. The builders had come and knocked right through the wall, and for a day or two the two rooms had been oddly connected and made one, the Finches' crowded, shabby little parlour and the Harpers' long, elegant sitting-room with its parquet floor and velvet curtains.

Not, of course, that the Finches had dreamed of using their parlour while only a tarpaulin sheet separated them from the Harpers. They had moved the television into the kitchen and lived there until the work was completed. The builders had then filled the arched gap with a sheet of hardboard, and decorators had been sent round to repaper the wall on the Finches' side. Else, Becky's mother, had been quite pleased about this, and chosen a new paper, one with blue roses and flecks of gold on it.

For a day or two afterwards there had been further banging and hammering on the Harpers' side of the wall while the shelves were being fixed, and after that, silence.

Or, at least, *comparative* silence. It did not seem to have occurred to Mrs Harper (who was slightly deaf as well as very impulsive) that a sheet of hardboard was not a very satisfactory form of walling between two separate dwellings. From last November the Finches had been able to hear, quite distinctly, every single word that had been spoken in the Harpers' sitting-room. The Harpers, on the other hand, were totally oblivious of this fact.

This was because the Finches, the moment the situation had become clear, had decided to keep the television in the kitchen, and whenever they used the parlour would sit conversing in loud whispers or even a kind of sign language that they had by now more or less perfected. If a cup so much as clinked in a saucer Else would wince as if stung, and Finch would turn the pages of his newspaper with elaborate care, peering anxiously over the top at Else's face as he did so.

At the same time, a straight-faced pretence was kept up that nothing at all had changed. Usually, Else crept into the parlour first to make sure that the coast was clear. If, however, the Harpers should later breeze into their sitting-room without warning, the Finches would carefully avoid looking at one another, and behave exactly as if each of them were stone deaf and believed the others to be so too. If the Harpers' conversation happened to take a particularly personal turn, Else would rise to her feet, whisper hoarsely 'Tea, Finch! Tea, Becky!' and jerk her head meaningfully towards the kitchen. The others would rise and troop obediently after her, taking care to close the door gently behind them, and making no reference whatever to the oddity of the proceedings.

By dint of these arrangements the Harpers had no inkling whatever of the situation, and the Finches themselves hardly liked to mention it, because by the time they had realized it, it had been too late.

'And she's that pleased with her shelves,' Else had told them, during the first week. 'Got all her best china arranged on the top ones, with a light on 'em, and his books at the bottom, and I must say it does look nice.'

Becky herself had grumbled a good deal about the arrangement during the first few weeks, especially as Christmas had been spent either sitting at the kitchen table or whispering themselves hoarse across the hearth in the parlour, without so much as daring to crack a nut. The tiny front room had a chimney that obstinately refused to carry away the smoke from a fire, so there was no question of using that.

Later, however, Becky had come to enjoy the situation hugely. She herself had no such scruples as her parents, and as both of them were often out, she spent many a happy hour eavesdropping on the unsuspecting Harpers. The only frustrating part about this was that although she gleaned many interesting items of information, she never dared repeat them to other people, and had to keep them strictly to herself. It was hard, but she managed it, knowing full well that the moment she talked the game would be up and over for ever.

She knew, for instance, a good deal more than she let on about the boy who was coming to stay.

13

She knew that his name was Jason, that he was twelve years old, and that he was extremely clever. She knew (which was probably more than he knew himself) that he would be spending the whole Easter holiday at the Harpers', and possibly the whole of the summer term at the village school. This was to give him 'some good country air' and to 'build him up'. She knew (and this, again, was possibly more than he knew himself) that his father was 'spineless' and that his mother had no taste whatsoever in either clothes or furnishings, that she had never read a good book in her life, that she had spoiled her son abominably, and that she 'spent money like water, just as her mother had done'. Becky had gathered that Jason's father was some kind of distant relation of Doctor Harper, and that Mrs Harper regretted this fact extremely, though she did not 'hold it against the boy'.

Nor was this all. As well as having a very good aural account of what was going on in the Harpers' sitting-room, Becky also had a very good visual one. She had, in fact, a secret spyhole.

This had come about on the second day of the hammering, when one of the carpenters had accidentally hammered right through the dividing partition. Becky herself had been in the parlour at the time, and her parents were out. She had looked up to see a hole appear in the newly decorated wall, about halfway up, and had immediately climbed up on to an armchair and put her eye to it. What she had seen, after a moment or two to focus, was what was unmistakably another human eye. Blue.

She had squealed and jumped down off the armchair, and a minute or two later the carpenter's face had appeared at the window.

'Have I made a mess?' he asked anxiously. 'What's it like your side?'

Becky had eyed the hole, meanwhile thinking rapidly. What she had thought, mainly, was A spyhole! A secret spyhole!

'Looks worse your side,' he had said, seeing it. 'Lot worse. New paper, and all. Now what?'

'Is it bad your side?' she had asked.

'It don't really *show*, our side. Only a little hole, and just under one of the shelves. You'd have to be looking for it—not even worth plugging. It's your new paper bothers me.'

'Don't worry! I'll fix it. There's a picture I can put over it. I'll get it now, and put it up before they get back, make out it's for a surprise.'

He had eyed her dubiously, and she had felt herself blush, ashamed despite herself.

'But it's as much to save him getting into trouble,' she had told herself, easing her conscience a little. She had run upstairs and fetched a picture of a boy in a green velvet suit blowing bubbles in a peeling gilt frame. It had lain on top of her wardrobe for as long as she could remember, along with several others that had belonged to her grandmother.

By the time the others returned, it had been tacked neatly into place by the chimney-breast.

'Do you like it?' Again she had felt a twinge of shame at their obvious surprise and pleasure.

'It goes a treat!' Else had cried warmly. 'Fancy her thinking of that, Finch! I'd all but forgot we had it, even! Always loved that, I did, since I was ever so little. It really takes me back, looking at it.'

And there the boy had been ever since, solemnly blowing his bubbles and looking straight into Becky's own eyes whenever she had lifted him down or tilted him to put her eye to the spyhole. She had come to feel a kind of kinship with him—they shared the same secret, were fellow-conspirators, almost.

He looked at her now as she knelt on the armchair and tilted him sideways. She wanted to check that Else, in a fury of spring-cleaning, had not fetched out all the books for dusting and put them back in the wrong order. If a tall volume were put in front of the hole, her view would be blocked, and today it was particularly important that it should not be.

Once before Else had put a volume of *Flowering Plants and Shrubs of the British Isles* right in Becky's line of vision, and it had been nearly a fortnight before Becky had had a chance to switch its position (on the pretext of helping out with the dusting). The volume over which she now peered, she saw with relief, was still the one she had put there herself—*Motoring Manual 1956*—which had seemed sufficiently dry and out of date to ensure that it was unlikely to be removed from the shelf.

She was about to drop the picture back into position when she caught sight, at the top of her field of vision, of a pair of shoes and legs that seemed familiar. Squinting, she saw that they belonged to her mother, who was evidently standing on a chair to dust something high up.

She's not put newspaper on the seat, thought Becky. She'll catch it if Mrs H. comes in.

At that very moment the feet disappeared and Else's middle portion came into view. Just in time. Almost instantaneously Mrs Harper's feet, in pink, fur-edged bedroom slippers, appeared behind her.

This was an aspect of the peephole that was at once intriguing and irritating. There were only one or two points in the room where people could be seen from head to foot, all over, as it were. Sometimes, if they sat in particular chairs, they disappeared altogether. In a way, it made the

business of spying more exciting and unpredictable. Becky would kneel there, eye glued to the hole, *willing* people to take up the right positions, and when, occasionally, they actually did so, it was oddly satisfying, as if she herself had been responsible and were working a kind of puppet-show.

'Oh—morning, Mrs Harper,' came Else's voice from her invisible lips. 'Just having a quick flick over.'

'Good morning, Elsie'—this from the bedroom slippers. 'I'm sure there's no need. I do feel sure that a boy of twelve years of age will not be checking to see whether or not there is dust on the chandeliers.'

'No. 'Course not, Mrs Harper.'

'And we did say scrambled eggs at seven?'

'Oh yes, yes—I'd lost all count of time—is it really that? Don't you worry, Mrs Harper, your breakfast shall be ready. You run off and get yourself dressed, and I'll have it on the table in no time.'

Becky wondered why Else, who was at least twenty years younger than Mrs Harper, always talked to her as though she were her mother.

The pink slippers turned away, stopped, then turned about again.

'Oh, and Elsie?'

'Yes, Mrs Harper?'

'About the boy. The doctor and I are not very used to children.'

'No, Mrs Harper.'

'And I rather think I'm a little nervous. I've taken in a good stock of breakfast cereals and lemonade, and I believe Finch has put up a swing in the large elm, but we are not at all sure, really, what . . .'

'Yes, Mrs Harper?'

'What we shall *do* with him, Elsie.'

The yellow duster made a generous, sweeping arc.

'Don't you go worrying about a single thing!' it cried. 'Bless his heart—I'll see he gets what he wants And he shall come and play with our Becky—she'll see he's all right.'

Oh will she? thought Becky. We'll see.

'Ah, well, that will be very nice.' The pink slippers sounded relieved. 'He's very intelligent, you know.'

At times like this, Becky wished the hole were big enough to enable her to stick her tongue through it. Instead, she let the picture swing back into place and plumped up the cushions on the armchair, covering her traces. As she left the room she heard Mrs Harper's voice, totally invisible now, saying something about packing. She stopped and pricked her ears.

'. . . possibly a month or two,' she heard. 'You know how it is with the doctor, he gets so wrapped up in—'

A door closed, cutting off the sentence in mid-air.

The doc's off again, thought Becky, returning to her cornflakes. The doc's off. To Timbuktoo, I shouldn't wonder, collecting date palms to cross with parsley. Or bananas with runner beans, or mangoes with—

At this point she quite forgot what it was she was thinking about, and gave her full attention to the cornflakes.

Chapter Three

'He *is* like forced rhubarb. With spectacles.'

Becky was sitting on her bed, watching the visitor help Finch heave his luggage from the car. He was taller than she had expected, even, and paler. The spectacles she had not bargained for at all.

'Thank you very much indeed.' His voice was high and clear and what the villagers were going to call 'posh'.

Next minute he was out of sight, a mere scrunch on the gravel.

Becky swung off the bed and ran downstairs to her next vantage point. Pushing the bubble boy unceremoniously aside and gluing her eye to the hole, she saw, with disappointment, that the sitting-room was empty. Faint voices told her that the visitor was being received elsewhere in the house.

'She probably won't let him in the sitting-room at all,' reflected Becky. 'The fuss she makes over her furniture and things.'

She allowed the picture to swing back into place, and as she did so, caught sight of her father and the doctor entering the working gardens through the arched gateway from Pew. The doctor was talking excitedly, waving his hands as if he were flapping off a gnat. Together they went into one of the lean-to greenhouses higher up the garden.

Becky went out, first taking a handful of corn from a bag behind the pantry door, and followed them. The doves flapped down for the flung corn. Inside the greenhouse she could see the doctor perched on a potting bench while Finch stood before him, nodding vigorously.

'Ah, Becky,' said the doctor. 'You'll have to meet our visitor, won't you? So you see, Finch, I think you ought to know the facts before I leave.'

'What you mean is, that you ain't sure *what* you've got.'

'What I mean is,' said the doctor, 'that the facts I am going to tell you, are not facts at all. All very disturbing. A fact must be a fact, Finch, or where should we all be?'

Finch was not given time to reply.

'You will recall that I attended a conference of the Botanical Society down in Margate in January?'

Nod.

'I met this fellow there. I got into a chat with

him on the last night, and he was saying he was just back from the Caucasus. I started to tell him about this crossing I'm doing down at Pew, and all of a sudden he cuts me short in mid-air and starts to wave this envelope at me. "I can see," says he, "that you are a man of imagination as well as a man of science." "I hope so," says I. "Then I beg you," says he, "that you will accept these as a gift!" and waves this under my nose.'

At this point he dug into his pocket and fetched out a blue airmail envelope.

'Now these, my dear Finch, are the seeds we have been raising this last week.'

'You mean those great long ones?' broke in Becky.

'And this is where the difficulty lies. Not only did he give me no indication whatever as to their origin, species, or habit, but I am having the utmost difficulty in recalling what his exact words *were* at this juncture.'

'You don't remember what he said,' prompted Finch.

'Exactly. It was all so *unbotanical*. I feel almost certain that he asked whether I were a *brave man*. Now why ever should he have done that?'

Finch shook his head.

'And as for the rest of what he said, it's gone completely. Dr Dunwig, who's Chairman this year, you know, came up with that Swedish horticulturalist who's just written that book on cross pollination, and this odd fellow pushed the envelope into my hand and was off.'

Finch said nothing, but stared at the airmail envelope.

'Didn't even get his name,' went on the doctor. 'Now what do *you* make of it all, Finch?'

Becky watched her father.

'It's interesting, sir,' he said at last. 'And, I should say, meant as a kind of compliment.'

'Compliment?'

'He gave it to *you*! sir, that's what I mean. As if he thought you were the right man for the job. And if I may say so, quite right too. It's coming along really extravagant, and a real credit to you.'

The doctor was frowning.

'But I don't know what it *is*, Finch,' he said. 'And the annoying thing is, I'm off tomorrow, and can't keep an eye on it. And this morning it didn't seem to me quite so *staunch* as I should like to see it. You know what I mean? Too much pliancy in the stem, a hint of pallor about the lower foliage. Did you notice?'

Becky's attention wandered. It often did, while the doctor was talking. It was not that she did not like him—and admire him, too, in a way. It was because he was so *flyaway*, so tricky with

24

words—too clever by half, she supposed. It seemed to Becky that the doctor was always *off* somewhere, always on wheels, always on trains, planes, voyages, always in *transit*. When he was at home, it was true, he spent most of the day in his laboratory and the Gardens. But even so, there was something she half mistrusted about his bookishness, his way of treating plants and flowers as though they were objects, rather than living things. He liked to dissect, to experiment, to discover. But the whole business seemed somehow to have nothing to do with the plants at all, as *plants*. It was as if he had been engaged for years on some kind of botanical paper-chase, and his fingers had lost their greenness along the way.

It was Finch, really, she thought, who was the true gardener. The doctor, for all his cleverness, had none of the wisdom that comes out of long green hours spent among things growing. Finch had soil under his nails and the rhythm of the seasons ran like a tide in his blood.

It's a wonder the doc ever knows what time of year it is, Becky thought. Rushing round the world from here to there, fetching back plants as if they were souvenirs. Winter one day, summer the next—how can he know what's going on at Pew? If Christmas came in July, *he'd* never notice. Pew's Dad's, not his!

Her attention went back to the conversation. By now the doctor was giving instructions for work to be carried out in his absence.

'And if you'll prepare the beds in the east forcing house,' he was saying, 'I should bring back enough specimens with me to furnish it. We'll use the compound we used for the *Passiflora quadrangularis* last year.'

Finch nodded.

'Oh—and you'd better have these.' He handed over the airmail envelope. 'I'll have to leave it entirely to you, Finch. Rely on your own judgement, as far as you can, but if you're in any doubt, just ring Dr Ainger, at Parklands. And don't test more than half—I should like to have another try myself when I get back.'

'I should like you to have a last look at the *Coccolus Carolinus* before you go, sir,' said Finch, taking the envelope.

They went out, deep in conversation, over to the far corner where Finch did his transplanting. Becky herself turned and went through the arch and into Pew Gardens proper—a thing she rarely did during the daytime.

A few visitors were strolling about the lawns, pausing here and there to admire or to consult their catalogues. A group of children were kicking a ball and she saw with a shudder that they were perilously near the *Rhexia virginica*—Finch's special pride and joy.

Can't they *read*? she thought, disgusted. If Dad catches them they're for it!

Finch was slow to anger, but roused had been known to frogmarch boys out of the gardens under the very eyes of their outraged parents, leaving them red-eared on the wrong side of the turnstiles.

Becky sauntered over towards the Tropical House, squinting sideways in the direction of the house for signs of the new arrival. When she reached the glasshouse, without really meaning to, she went inside for the second time that day, and made her way automatically towards the centre. She saw that the cloches had been removed since the morning and, staring again at the seedlings, wondered whether she were only imagining that they had grown a foot or so taller since last she had seen them.

Like weeds, she thought. That was what Finch always said—'You can't beat a weed for making growth.'

He used to tell her it was a natural law—the survival of the fittest—and that if all the gardeners were to lay down their spades tomorrow, there would be nothing but buttercups and chickweed between Lands End and John O' Groats within a twelvemonth.

Look well if it *was* a weed, she thought, and the doc treating it as if it was an orchid, or something!

She let out a giggle at the thought—she could not help herself—and looking up, met the stare of a boy standing directly opposite, on the other side of the little stone island. It was *the* boy.

Becky, furious with herself, face burning, tried to smile. It might not have been a very successful attempt, she later told herself, but at least it deserved more than the brief stare she received— and, a moment later, the turned back.

'Oh!' she whispered savagely after his retreating back. 'Oh!'

She herself turned and made for the door, suffocated with heat and humiliation. So that was what he was like, she thought, outside. Just as she had known he would be—stuck-up, rude, superior.

Thinks he owns Pew already, does he? she thought. We'll see about that, Master Brainy Jason!

It did not even occur to her that there was a very simple explanation for what had just happened. In the first place, what she had thought was a smile had not been a smile at all, but a kind of furious grimace. And in the second, Becky (by dint of her spying) had known exactly who Jason was, but he had never set eyes on her before in his life. To him, she had simply been a red-faced, grimacing stranger who was probably in the middle of choking on a boiled sweet, and he had done the politest thing he could think of in the circumstances—tried not to stare, and turned away.

And so Becky, who was not a born spy, only rudely and incurably curious, made the fateful mistake that was to let loose upon Pew a kind of wild green doom. And she had not meant it like that at all. She had not meant it at all.

Chapter Four

Within twenty-four hours Becky had found the form her revenge would take. When the idea did occur to her, it was so deliciously neat and simple that she was amazed to think that she had lain awake for several hours the night before without so much as touching its fringe. Not that it was really the kind of thing you could plan. It happened so naturally that it might almost have been meant.

The following afternoon she was in one of the lean-to greenhouses watching Finch re-potting plants. She was in there not because she wanted to be—it was much too hot, and she was bored—but because a few minutes earlier Else had suggested that she could go and find Jason.

'You could take him down the village,' she had said. 'Get him into the hang of things.'

'I promised I'd give Dad a hand,' Becky had lied swiftly. 'Later, Mum. There's plenty of time.'

But she had been leaning against the bench watching Finch's slow, square fingers for barely ten minutes when the door opened and Jason stepped inside.

Becky was instantly affronted. It was absurd, she realized, to expect anyone to knock at a greenhouse door, but to walk in, without so much as a cough or a rattle of the knob, as if he owned it . . .

'Hello,' he said, just standing there.

'Hello.' She jumped up on to the bench and swung her legs, never taking her eyes off Finch. Finch merely turned his head and nodded.

'I came to see if I could give a hand,' he said. 'Aunt Delia thought I might. And I think I could get rather interested, though I don't know much about it yet.'

Again Finch made no reply. This, Becky knew, was not rudeness, it was merely because he had not yet decided *what* to reply.

'I'm not bad at picking things up,' Jason added.

Finch straightened.

'There's no harm in your learning,' he said then. 'It's where to start you. Can't have any mistakes made in this garden, d'ye see.'

'No, of course not,' said Jason. 'I can see that. People paying to come in, and that.'

Finch stared, as though this thought had only just occurred to him. Other people came into his reckoning hardly at all.

'I'll tell you what, then,' he said. 'Becky'll take

you and show you our garden, out at the front
there. Make a start there, will you, and we'll see
how you shape?'

Jason nodded and looked enquiringly at Becky,
who was glaring murderously at Finch.

'You take Jason to the toolshed, Becky,' he
ordered, 'and you can lay out a couple of beds for
seeding. I've got to go into Selling, later, for
compost, but I'll leave the packets out here for
you on the bench.'

Glumly Becky climbed down from her perch.

'Come on,' she said ungraciously, and they went
out.

The Finches had a small garden of their own,
lying to the front and side of the house. By some
unspoken agreement it was Else and Becky who
looked after it and had chosen all the trees and
shrubs. The result was an odd, exotic mixture of
the English and the sub-tropical, of a cottage
garden and a mid-African jungle. Rubber plants
rubbed shoulders with stock and marigolds, and
the thoroughly English thrush nested yearly in a
North American tulip tree. It was, in fact, a
private extension of Pew itself, only not so formal,
and with a happy-go-lucky, individual flavour that
came of being tended by gardeners who saw no
harm in screening a dustbin with twitch, and
training clematis up monkey trees.

Else and Finch never could see eye to eye over weeds.

'Weeding a garden is same as dusting in a house, Else,' he would tell her, time and again, shaking his head over the banks of weeds that seemed to gather in her own garden like fugitives, refugees from the grim war waged upon them in Pew itself. 'You got to do it regular.'

'Nonsense!' Else would reply. 'Weeds like *dust*? Now, Finch, you never believe that! Weeds is lovely, some of 'em, prettiest things out. *I* can't find it in my heart to murder 'em, and I'm surprised *you* can.'

So the weeds stayed, except for occasional victims in the spring, when Else would clear and replant her borders the minute she had done all the jobs she could think of inside the house. This year, that time had not yet arrived, and it occurred to Becky with glee that Jason had fallen right into the weeding.

The whole point about weeding in Else's garden, was that you only weeded out the *weeds*, so to speak, the ones Else called the *real* weeds—ones that could be roughly defined as being either without much of a flower, or with a sting. What this usually boiled down to was groundsel, and nettles.

'You do that bed, will you?' said Becky, waving

an arm towards the centre bed, Else's favourite, that later in the season would be a riot of dandelions and marigolds, and later still, of campion and delphinium. 'You do know *how* to weed?'

'Should do,' replied Jason. 'If in doubt, pull 'em out—that's what we always say.'

'*Here*,' said Becky, 'we say the exact opposite.'

'Really?' Jason stared. 'What, you mean sort of if in doubt, let 'em sprout?'

Becky almost giggled. If Jason had been friend instead of foe, she almost certainly would have done.

'I s'pose,' she said instead, turning away to pick up a hoe.

'Hey, that's not bad,' said Jason. 'I just made that one up. If in doubt—let 'em sprout!'

Becky pretended not to hear. Later, she heard him mutter:

'It'd be easier *later* in the year, when you can see which *are* weeds.'

But most of the time all she heard was the steady thrust of his spade into the soil. She deliberately did not look, so that if he did dig up the wrong things, she could not be blamed.

She became so absorbed in her own work that she did not notice when the digging stopped, and was startled by Jason's voice, right beside her.

'I've finished,' he said. '*You've* left a lot of

stuff in, haven't you? Buttercups are weeds, you know.'

He sounded faintly scornful.

'Not here, they're not,' replied Becky. 'We choose our *own* weeds.'

'Where're the seeds, anyway?' he asked.

'Dad said he'd leave them on the bench. You'll see 'em. In envelopes, with the names written on.'

She heard him scrunch off over the gravel. He was back within a few minutes.

'These them?'

She looked up. He was waving a fistful of brown envelopes. Among them, unmistakable

with its dark blue and red edging, was an airmail envelope.

It was then that the idea had come to her. It came, took root and blossomed, all in an instant. She hesitated for only a second.

'Those are them.'

'What shall I do with them? Shall I use half, and leave you half?'

She nodded.

'Just sprinkle 'em here and there,' she told him. 'Don't bother about rows, or anything. Mum likes 'em like that—artistic.'

Her mind was dancing and alarmed, both together. Wouldn't he catch it? But what seeds *were* they? Never mind—wait till Finch found out—and Mum, with all her buttercups murdered to boot! Did it really matter—about the seeds? She wouldn't use her half, then there would be some left. It couldn't be her fault, could it—*could* it? Oh, Jason, you've gone and cooked your goose proper!

When he came up to hand over the half-empty envelopes she found herself smiling at him for the first time, happy in the thought that he had sown his own doom with his very own hands.

'I wasn't too sure what this one was.' He was holding out the airmail envelope. Her heart jumped a beat. 'But I sowed it anyway. There weren't many, and I've used them all, I'm afraid. What is it?'

'Oh, that,' she heard herself saying carelessly. 'Probably the South American Bongleweed.' It was the first name that came into her head—it came so easily, right out of the blue, that she almost believed in it herself.

'Oh, *very* likely,' Jason said. She felt her face burn.

Thinks I've made it up, does he? she thought. We'll soon see who's clever, Master Jason Harper!

Swiftly she scattered her own seeds, carelessly, with Finch fingers, fingers confidently green.

'There's this old woman in Brum,' came Jason's voice softly from behind her, 'reckons she's a witch.'

Had not Becky been feeling guilty, perhaps the hairs would not suddenly have stirred along her neck. She began to brush the earth over the seeds with her fingers with a light, pressing movement as Finch had taught her.

'Get your *fingers* into it,' he was always saying. 'Never mind the trowel. It's the *fingerwork* that matters.'

'Did you hear what I said?' It was Jason again, still behind her, with his shadow falling over the seeds she had planted.

'Yes,' she replied, sweeping, pressing, kneading the damp soil. 'What's her name?'

'Mrs Crump.'

'I know a witch called Mrs Crump!' said Becky to herself, and wanted to giggle. Out loud she said:

'Witches aren't Mrs anything. They have *names*— like Sabina or Esmeralda. Either that, or no name at all.'

'Her name is Mrs Crump,' repeated Jason. 'She's *got* a first name, if you want to know.'

'What?'

'Daisy.'

Becky did giggle then, she could not help herself.

'All right. I thought you might be interested. Witches don't grow on trees, you know.'

'Oh, I know,' agreed Becky. She scrambled to her feet.

'And why would she say she was, if she wasn't?'

'Yes, why?' agreed Becky again.

'All right. Forget it!' He turned and swung off.

'No—I—' She found herself starting after him and when he turned to face her she actually looked at him, square in the face, for the first time. It was a mistake, she knew that in the instant. As long as she had not met his eyes she could think of him as the Enemy—a faceless foe. Now he was a person, and not really bad at all—she felt a swift compunction about the seeds, about the mean trap she had let him fall into.

'Go on,' she said, 'tell me.'

They began to walk round the house and back to the work garden.

'Nothing to tell. She said she was a witch, that's all.'

'*Is* she, do you think?'

He shrugged.

'Mother believes in her. Goes every month to get her cards read. *She* calls her a clairvoyant.'

'I expect that's what she is, then.' Becky felt unaccountably relieved. After all, there was no reason why she, strolling in the broad sunshine at Pew, should care about an old woman in Brum called Crump, witch or not.

'*And* a witch,' said Jason with unexpected emphasis.

Becky, surprised, stopped in her tracks. She had thought the subject was closed.

'You don't actually believe in them do you? Not *actually*—outside of books, and that?'

'Oh, I know that there aren't such things in a way,' he said. 'Grown *ups* don't believe in them, and even if they do they give them another name—like clairvoyant. But you've got to keep an open mind.'

'Oh, you have,' agreed Becky, wondering if he were slightly mad. Supposed to be so clever, she thought, and here he was talking about witches as if he was six years old.

'Old Parker—that's this master at my school—says we must always keep an open mind. I do. I believe in *everything*.'

'But only if you can prove it,' said Becky. 'Or at any rate know it for certain—in your bones, sort of.'

'I do know it,' he said. 'She's a witch.'

'All right,' said Becky. 'She is, then. Shall we go down to the village?'

They went down to the village, and that was the end of the witch from Brum.

Chapter Five

Becky could not sleep that night. She had read for a while and then put out the light and turned over, but instead of seeing against her eyelids the usual drowsy procession of pictures that carried her into sleep, she found herself absolutely wide awake, alert, almost, as if waiting for something. It was an effort even to close her eyes, and in the end she just lay there staring at the pattern on her curtains lit from behind by the moon.

After a long while she heard her parents come up, and closed her eyes while her mother entered and leaned over her, giving her blankets a final tweak.

'Goodnight,' she heard Else say softly. 'God bless.'

Becky had heard her mother say this on previous occasions when she had lain and feigned sleep, and supposed that Else came in and went through the same ritual every night over her sleeping form. She had never thought very much about it before, it had seemed a perfectly natural thing.

But tonight, when the door closed quietly and

Becky's eyes opened again, she found herself repeating the formula over and over again as if searching for some kind of meaning in it.

Almost as if she thought we'd never meet again, Becky thought. As if it were *dangerous* to go to bed and go to sleep, as if she were going on some kind of voyage, might be journeying into perilous places. Not that it really meant anything. She often heard it said. God bless my soul! If you haven't got a penny a ha'penny will do if you haven't got a ha'penny, God bless you. It meant nothing at all. Bless you every time you sneezed . . . Nothing at all.

Bless, bless, bless . . .

Becky sat bolt upright in bed, listening intently. There it was again. Bless, bless, bless . . . A whispering, a hissing like wind in poplars, a conspiracy of leaves. But the only tree near Becky's window was a monkey puzzle—and monkey puzzles neither sigh nor whisper nor even moan— they are silent, keeping their own counsel. Bless, bless, bless . . .

Becky looked over towards the window. The curtains hung motionless, there was not so much as a stir in a draught.

'There's some perfectly simple explanation.' She whispered the words out loud. 'Perfectly simple explanation.'

It was one of Doctor Harper's favourite phrases and it usually, she was bound to admit, turned out to be true.

But tonight? There it was again—bless, bless . . . Or was it wish, wish . . . or again us, us, us . . .

Whichever? thought Becky, *who*ever? Down there, in the moonlight? Whoever? And why?

Bless wish us . . . bless wish us . . .

No harm in looking. Becky was used to spying through spyholes. She threw back the blankets, went over to the window and parted the curtains ever so slightly. She put her left eye to the slit and squinted.

So close now was the blessing and wishing and hushing and so dense and criss-crossing as if from a thousand voices, that at first she could focus on nothing at all. Mile upon mile of moonlight lay blank and unpeopled. Then slowly the garden began to make itself under her eyes, fragments of dark and light sorted themselves into recognizable patterns. There was the yew and there the dustbin and there the silver square of Mr Fowler's roof and the misted curve of the hill beyond. But below, right under the very sill it seemed, the voices remained invisible as ever, and insistent.

Becky, bolder now that the world outside was still there the same as ever, lifted the casement latch and pushed the window wider. She stuck out her head so that part of her at least was right out there, full in the silvery garden—cold as it was, and she felt the stir of gooseberry pimples under her thin nightdress.

Now that she was right in the midst of it all, oddly enough the voices were neither louder nor clearer nor in any way easier to decipher. She was not even sure now that they were either blessing or hushing or anything else. She was not even certain that they were voices at all. On a wild night with a raggedy wind she could have put the whole thing down to the shaking of leaves. She could have told herself 'The poplars are in good voice tonight', and gone straight back to bed. After all, Pew was a place of trees, and many a night she had lain and fancied herself at sea.

What she *did* have, now that her head was hanging out into the absolutely still, moonlit air, was a feeling of enormous *stir* and excitement. The whispers were voices gossiping—more, they were telling secrets. Hush—listen—hush—the uncannily still and silver garden was alive with conspiracies beyond all guessing.

Guess . . . guess . . . listen . . . hush . . .

The three-quarters moon hung blank and imperturbable—poker-faced, the sure-as-eggs ringleader of it all. Becky banged the window and pulled the curtains fiercely back into place. Lying in bed again she found herself trembling, more with rage than anything else. Becky was a tricker by nature, and a tricker hates nothing so much as to be tricked.

The whispering went on but she would not go to the window again. She would not give *them*—whoever they were—the satisfaction of even seeming to be tricked. She fumed and grew hotter under blankets pulled up over her head and in the end (for want of a better solution) fell asleep.

Her mother had to wake her in the morning, and the whole day started on the wrong foot—to be *told* to wake up, as if it were not a thing one could do perfectly well by oneself, given sufficient time.

Balefully she glared out of the window as she pulled on her jeans and shirt. Almost without thinking she opened the window, half expecting a chorus of whispers to blow in with the birdsong. Hastily she shut it. The wind was bitter and in the east. The whispering was all over—blown out. She pulled a jersey over her shirt. If it had ever *been* there, in the first place.

'Dreaming,' she told herself scornfully. Almost immediately, dragging the brush across her hair, she felt depressed. A mystery come and a mystery gone—just like that—overnight. If the whispers *had* been real, what a day *this* would have been, east wind, scribbled charcoal clouds and all!

'What's one thing at night's another in the morning.'

Her grandmother had always been saying that.

And what a pity *that* is, Becky thought, and went down to breakfast.

Chapter Six

The doves were hunched into their feathers, detesting the wind. Becky flung them their three handfuls of corn and they took the plunge then—fluttered down from the ledge, letting the cold into their feathers.

'Where's that boy?' she wondered, and went to look.

She met him head on by a large laurel. It was on the Finches' side of the fence.

'Hello! What're you doing here?'

He looked surprised.

'What are you?' he countered.

'It's our garden,' she said pointedly.

'Oh. Trespassing, am I? Didn't see a notice.'

Clever, thought Becky. So *he* thinks.

She remembered the seeds and a smile spread. Jason, thinking it was meant for him, grinned, and instantly she checked it.

'Let's see how the seeds we planted are getting on,' she said.

'What for? They won't be up for days. Weeks.'

'I know *that*.' She led the way to the front of the house. She wanted to gloat, to see again the bed where he had murdered Else's best weeds and sown his own doom.

'Oooooh!' The gasp flew from her lips of its own accord.

'Where *was* it?' came Jason's voice.

Dumbly she shook her head. Shock had her by the throat. Up in the night—two feet, three?—reared by the moon, and whispering while they waxed . . .

I've done it now, she found herself thinking. O sweet mystery of life, I've done it now!

'It was here!' Jason's voice again. 'No. Couldn't have been. Where on earth. . . ?'

What were they? What? She stared at the springing green of them for clues and meanings. They were not just tall, they had grown dense and tangling, intricate as ivy. They had spread. They were going to creep.

'Oh no!' she said out loud. 'Not *creep*!'

'It *was* here,' said Jason. 'So who's been putting these other things in on top of them?'

'Damn! Oh damn!' said Becky under her breath.

'Who *has*?'

'Don't keep going *on*!' she turned on him now. 'Just shut up and pull 'em up!'

'Pull them *up*?'

Savagely she grasped one and tugged. She fell
back in a shower of soil. With a mixture of bliss
and awe she stared at the plant in her hand, then
let it drop sharply. Something in her could not
bring herself to finger it lightly. She suspected it.

'Come on—help!' she told Jason. He shrugged
and began to pull in turn. Becky tugged and
dropped, tugged and dropped. She worked rapidly,
holding her breath. When they all lay uprooted,
then she let it out, in one long gasp.

'Now what?'

'Wheelbarrow,' said Becky briefly. 'Compost
heap.'

There were three journeys with the wheelbarrow.

The plants waved springy arms as they rode to the dump and Becky still suspected them. What she suspected them of she did not know—unless, perhaps, it was of being still alive.

'Can't be,' she told herself, huffing over the final load. 'Dead as dodos. Down among the dead men . . .'

Between the rusted iron bars of the high railings she glimpsed the stone wings of an angel, and grinned.

'Down among the dead men—let them lie!'— and upended the wheelbarrow.

'That the graveyard through there?' said Jason. 'I wouldn't like a graveyard at the bottom of my garden.'

'Ghosts, I suppose,' said Becky, setting off back. 'First witches, now ghosts!'

'Yawning graves. Slabs heaving at the stroke of twelve. No thanks!'

'That's all right,' she said. 'No one's offering it you. I've never seen a grave yawn in my whole life. Though come to think of it, being dead must be pretty boring. You couldn't *blame* a grave yawning.'

'Look,' he said, 'I'll go, if you like. Unless there's any more gardening to do. Unless there're any more plants that have sprung up in the night and want pulling up.'

Becky stopped instantly.

'What do you mean, "sprung up in the night"?' she said.

'*Those* did, didn't they?'

She was silent.

'Go on,' he said. 'Say "It's impossible".'

'Well, it is,' she said at length.

'It happened, though.'

Again she was silent.

'Well? Didn't it?'

They faced one another. She looked right through his spectacles and into his eyes. She even noticed his eyelashes. He was having a good look at her, too, and she blushed for her past rudenesses.

'I'm sorry,' she said. 'Let's start again.'

He nodded, and she saw that he knew exactly what she meant, that it was going to be possible to talk to him properly now, say things she really meant, drop the mask. She let fall the handles of the wheelbarrow and they went into the potting shed.

'You knew they'd come up overnight,' he said, after a time.

'Yes. At least, almost. But how did you? How could you possibly? Things *don't*.'

'Simple,' he told her. 'Yesterday they weren't there, today they were. Two and two always make four, even if four's an impossible answer.'

She looked at him.

'But you knew, even without working it out,' he persisted. She felt the heat rise in her face again.

'All right, I'll tell you,' she said.

She was glad now of the dry, confessional smell of the place, eager to tell her sins. He listened well, without interruption, without even expression. She confessed everything, and by the time she had finished was lightheaded with relief, and felt she would have gone through fire for him.

'Is your father going to miss those seeds?' he asked.

She shook her head.

'It's all over then, isn't it? No one'll ever know. Except us.'

'And them.'

She spoke without thinking, without even knowing what she meant. Then she told him about the voices, the whispers in the moonlight. All the time she was talking, she knew it was the truth she was telling him. Strangely, the very act of telling it *made* it the truth.

'Do you believe me?' she asked.

'Of course. Why should you make it up? Besides, it fits.'

'Fits? What?'

She strained after the comfortable cooing of

well-fed doves outside, a background noise of reassurance she had known from her cradle.

'Everything. You don't imagine those were ordinary seeds, do you?'

Dumbly she shook her head—Finch all over, for the moment.

'Well—what kind?'

Again she shook her head, not meaning to, but helpless.

'Magic,' Jason said.

The doves had let her down. She let out a long-held breath, one she had not even realized she *was* holding.

'All right,' she said at last. 'Magic.'

And now that it had been said, that too was true, and she felt a huge, racing excitement stronger than anything she had ever felt in her life before. If the shed had shuddered into splinters at that moment, or if she herself had taken to the air, or if a tall genie had shot up with a flash of light from one of Finch's plantpots, she would have felt not the least surprise. In fact, it seemed only fitting at that moment that one, at least, of those things *should* happen. And when it did not, and when the excitement began to ebb and she was conscious of the doves outside again, and the dry smell of creosote, she felt oddly cheated, left flat. Jason was looking at her.

'That's better,' he said. 'And witches?' She swallowed and nodded. Anything could happen.

'Mrs Crump of Brum?' he persisted ruthlessly.

Reduced to Finchlikeness again, she nodded.

'The worst of it is,' Jason mused, 'that we've gone and spoilt it now. We ought to have left them. Now we'll never know what would've happened.'

'We could—put them back?' suggested Becky. But fear and excitement were at war even as she spoke. She knew perfectly well that nothing in the world would induce her to go back, lift one of those springing, rubbery plants and press it back into the earth. Jason was shaking *his* head now.

'No good. That's no good. Like trying to put the clock back. I mean, you can move the fingers on a clock, but you can't move the time. *That* wouldn't do any good.'

'I suppose not.' She tried to sound sorry.

He swung his legs down.

'I suppose there's one thing we can do. We can go and have a look at the others, the ones in the glasshouse.'

They crossed the wide, windswept lawns and Jason said, 'Any signs of the roof coming off?'

And despite herself Becky's eyes went straight to the tropical house, half expecting to see it crowned with a towering spiral of green, like a hat with a plume.

'I mean, if they grow like that in the moonlight, think what a bit of sun on 'em'll be doing,' he said, and hastened his step.

The tropical house was as usual—breathtakingly hot wet air, endless dripping and trickling of water— a vulgarity of life and greenness.

'Bongleweed my foot!' Becky heard Jason say under his breath and then they were right at the greenmost heart of the glass-bound jungle and there it was, in front of them. They stopped and stared.

'But it's hardly grown at all!' Becky cried. 'In fact—in fact it's—!'

'Go on,' he said, 'say it. It's shrunk!'

'Oh no! Not shrunk! But it doesn't look, it looks *weedy* somehow . . .' She recalled Doctor Harper's words to Finch. 'Not so staunch,' she finished.

There was a faint, yellowish tinge about the foliage, a suspicion of pallor and droop that Becky had come to recognize as the signs of failure, as prelude to the final resigned shrug of Finch's shoulders, the merciless uprooting, the patient starting all over again. Even Finch failed sometimes. Perhaps that was why he was so patient.

'So in other words,' came Jason's voice, 'they've just about had it?'

'Well—' she hesitated. 'I don't know about

that. They just don't look so good. Dad'll perhaps be able to do something. There's all kinds of things . . .' she trailed off.

'Not with these,' Jason said. 'Nothing out of a bottle's going to do anything for *them*. They'll probably go up in a puff of green smoke at any minute.'

Alarmed in the muffled, breathing jungle, Becky clutched at his arm.

'Come on. No point standing here. What about swimming? We could go swimming. Take a bus. Come on, Jason, let's go.'

He came. At the door she gulped in the windy air with more than usual relief. She started to run.

End of the chapter, she thought.

Chapter Seven

Becky tried not to go down to the compost heap next morning. But when her mother had gone next door to see to the breakfast and Finch was already out on his first round of the gardens, the house, it seemed to her, had more than its ordinary early morning stillness. It seemed full of silence and ticking clocks.

'The older clocks are, the louder they tick,' she thought. All the clocks in their house were old. They had ticked the time away for grandmothers and great-grandmothers, and even further back for what she supposed would be called 'ancestors', the ones who lay under mossed and crooked stones in the graveyard beyond the rusting iron gate by the compost heap.

Her thoughts had turned full circle again. Compost heap.

May as well go and look, she thought. No harm. Just a lot of withered old weeds.

She went out, exchanging the old brown smell of the kitchen for the wet overnight odours of the

57

garden, powerfully rising from the green. In a week or less the cuckoos would be calling and then it would all be perfect.

The compost heap had disappeared. Becky was not surprised. She had already seen in her mind's eye the scene that now lay before her. Last night as she lay in bed her thoughts had run wild and had clothed the corner of the garden in a riot of foliage. She had seen the iron railings of the graveyard changed overnight to a towering wall of green. She had seen a madness of greenery, she had seen it tumbling north, south, east, and west and spiralling up towards the sky. Then she had almost laughed out loud at the picture, had turned over and gone to sleep.

And there it was. She stood and stared at it, and so powerful a feeling of life did the plants give out that it seemed not at all unlikely that they were staring back.

Cat's out of the bag, thought Becky. No hiding *this* lot.

She went straight back to the house to wait for her mother and father. She did not stay, for fear that she would actually see the Bongleweed grow.

Else was back first. She was clearly in a bad temper.

'I shall *kill* that fish man, before I'm finished,' she announced, banging her handbag on the table among the breakfast things and unpinning her hat. (She always wore her hat to go next door. Pinned it on, went out the back door, round through the garden gate to the Harpers' back door, into the kitchen, *un*pinned it, and the day's work had begun.)

'It's like trying to make sense to a *foreigner*!' she went on now, filling the kettle, fetching out cups and saucers. 'Finny haddock for two I tell him— over the phone, mind you, only yesterday—and six nice plaice fillets for company tonight. I could scream, Becky, I really could.'

'So what happened?' enquired Becky, guessing already.

'What you might *think'd* happen,' replied Else grimly. 'Two plaice fillets and six bits of finny haddock as tatty as ever I saw. I've brought a couple back for you, Becky. And I shall have to get the bus into Selling and fetch the plaice myself, and if I don't tell that fishy little Welshman what I think of him and his finny haddock, my name's not Elsie Finch.'

Becky was cheered by her mother's bad temper. She knew her well enough to know that a ramping, raving Bongleweed in the garden would rate as a mere second-class disaster by comparison with a domestic crisis over the fish.

She was about to take advantage of this fact to

tell Else straight away about the seeds, when Finch came in. He looked not so much bad-tempered—he was never that—as glum. Becky's heart sank. Something had gone wrong in Pew. And now she had to tell him that something else was wrong—wronger than anything else could possibly be.

Finch removed his cap and sat at the table, shaking his head as if engaged in silent conversation with himself.

'Something wrong, Dad?' Becky asked.

He looked up.

'Aye.' There was a pause. Then again, 'Aye.'

'Badly wrong?' she persisted.

Another pause, as if he were trying to be absolutely fair to the situation—whatever it was.

'Not exactly,' he said at last. 'More a disappointment, Becky. A disappointment.'

Once he had *found* the right words, Finch was often tempted to repeat them.

'We're *all* disappointed,' Becky heard her mother mutter. 'This morning, we're *all* disappointed.'

Finch continued to sit there, looking, Becky thought for the thousandth time, like a fish out of water. Indoors, he always looked out of place and oddly ill at ease, as if his green fingers did not know what to do with themselves away from greenery.

'You'll know what I mean, Becky,' he said. 'You heard the doctor talk about them seeds.'

'W-w-which seeds, Dad?' Her heart stopped dead. He knew.

'What you might call the *anonymous*,' he went on. 'Them I had in the tropical house, in that centre island.'

'Oh. Oh—them.'

Silence. Nod.

'Them!' Her voice came out an octave higher this time.

'Gone,' said Finch gloomily.

Gone? Walked off? *Kidnapped?* Or not—surely not—?

'Dead,' Finch confirmed. 'Suddenest falling off I've ever known. Flat on their backs. One minute up in the air like Indian rope tricks, next flat.'

'Really?' she cried. '*Really!* Dad?'

She remembered the visit to the Jungle House the day before, with Jason, and how even then the plants had seemed to be yellowing and wilting, as if after that first tremendous spurt they had outgrown their strength and given up. 'Outgrown his strength . . .' She remembered how Finch had used this very phrase about Jason, and how she had scoffed at the idea. But now, wildly searching for a way out, she saw even Finch's disaster as a hope. If *his* seeds had come to grief, perhaps he might even be glad to know that she herself had had success with them—if success was the word.

Whether or not, she took a deep breath and plunged straight in.

'Had a bit better luck, myself,' she announced boldly, switching boats in midstream. She had been going to make a confession. Now she decided to claim a victory.

'Luck!' she heard her mother mutter. 'I don't believe in luck, not this morning.'

But Finch was listening. He didn't say anything, of course, just looked and waited.

'*I've* got some Bongleweed,' she announced.

His face was blank.

'That's what I call it,' she went on. 'Bongleweed. Got to have a *name* for things, haven't you? It's in the back, Dad, down by the churchyard. And it was only an accident, Dad, it just *happened*. It's how I know it's a weed—just like you're always saying. You can't stop it!'

Still he looked—or rather the look had deepened now, into a stare.

'I tried to stop it. Pulled it up by its roots and threw it on the compost, and it's only two days and you should—'

'I'm off now,' announced Else. The hat was on again, planted square and low, a sure sign of her mood. 'If you could rely on the *buses*, it'd help!'

They turned vaguely and watched her go. When the door banged behind her Becky could hear the clocks ticking again and had lost the thread of what she had been saying. She simply could not go on.

The door opened again and they both looked up. Else stood there, her face scarlet.

'And what're those trees doing there?' she half screamed. 'It's too bad, Finch! You pull 'em out again, do you hear?'

'I hear, Else,' said Finch mechanically. His stare was glassy now. Nothing that had been said in the last few minutes had meant anything to him at all. He was beginning to doubt his own senses, Becky could see that.

'Well—do!' Else cried. A thrusting gesture with the black plastic shopping bag, and she was gone. The clocks came back into their own again. Becky stared down at the tablecloth and saw a tea stain and wondered how old it was and whose fault it had been and whether her father had been listening to a single word she had been saying and whether the only thing to do now was to run away from home.

Finch got up and cleared his throat.

'Better go and look,' he said, almost as if hoping to be contradicted.

Silently Becky followed him. They walked round the side of the house and saw the trees, and stopped.

They were not trees, exactly. They did not have trunks or anything that was recognizably tree-like, except their size. They were simply—growths. Or overgrowths.

We missed some, Becky thought dully. Oh sweet mystery of life!

Finch, it seemed, was rooted. She glanced sideways at him but could only guess at the thoughts that were turning slowly under that frayed cap. Finch's face did not go *in* for expressions.

The silence went on for so long that she took another look. He had his eyes closed.

'He doesn't believe them!' she realized. 'He's *testing* them!'

Finch's eyes opened again, warily.

'You see, Becky, it don't seem possible,' he said at last. 'You'll be seeing them yourself?'

'Yes, Dad. I see them.'

She realized that he did not connect what he was looking at with what she had just been telling him—or, indeed, connect them with her at all. The worst—the confession—was still to come.

'They'll be about fifteen foot,' Finch's voice went on. 'Wouldn't you say, Becky?'

'About that, Dad.'

Side by side they stood and looked. What had sprung up over Else's best flower patch, over the buttercups and dandelions and last year's sweet williams, was a kind of jungle.

'It's upset your mother, I could see that.'

She did not answer.

'Upset me,' he added, after a long pause.

'Dad . . .' said Becky in a small voice. She tugged at his sleeve and he turned unthinkingly and began to follow her back, past the cottage, down through the work garden, beyond the potting sheds.

There they stopped. It was still there—more there than *ever* it seemed to Becky. And yet now, now that the worst was nearly over and Finch himself was seeing it, she found to her amazement that she wanted to laugh. She wanted to laugh and cry with delight at the sheer nerve, the life, the *cheek* of the thing, with its careless lack of consideration for walls, boundaries, rules—even for the laws of nature. And for a weed to go mad in Pew, Pew of all places, was the most glorious touch of all.

With a sudden rush of affection she realized that she *loved* it, found it bold and splendid beyond anything she had ever known.

'There!' she cried. 'There it is, Dad! Isn't it marvellous? It's the Bongleweed!'

'Bongleweed, Becky?' He repeated her words mechanically more as if he were using them as a

straw to clutch at than actually taking them in. She remembered her own first shock, and sympathized.

'I told you, Dad. That's my name for it. But it's those seeds, Dad. You know—the doctor's. The ones you said had fallen flat on their faces in the night. *These*'ll never fall flat on their faces!'

She looked up at the weed with something like pride now.

I've got green fingers, too! she thought. Greener than green!

She looked sideways and saw that Finch was shaking his head again. Staring and shaking. Then he turned and began to walk steadily in the direction of the sheds, steadily but blindly, like a practised sleepwalker.

With a swift, involuntary wave, a kind of salute, to the Bongleweed, Becky followed and caught up.

'Where're you going?'

'Sprays.' He was still walking. 'Selective weed-killer. That'll see it off. Double concentration, and never mind if it sees the ivy off as well. That'll be it.'

'Dad, no!'

The words were out before she even had time to think. She had hardly realized how suddenly and completely she was on the side of the Bongleweed now.

'It's the doctor's experiment, Dad!' she cried. 'And it's working!'

He stopped so suddenly that she overtook him and had to turn back to face him. She saw that his eyes had lost some of their glazed purposefulness, and pressed home her advantage.

'The other lot've died. These are our last chance now. If you kill these off—'

She left the sentence unfinished. He was nodding now. Her point had been taken.

'They're not doing any harm, Dad, not down there. You never *grow* anything in that corner. And think what Doctor Harper'll say when he sees it! I bet he'll never've seen anything like it in his life! It'll make *history*, Dad!'

'Botanical,' nodded Finch. For him there *was* no other kind of history.

'All kinds of history!' sang Becky. 'Beautiful weed, beautified weed, beautiful pea-green weed!'

She stared up at it and saw how deliciously new and green it was and the sun was lathering it with gold and the magic of the thing was plain to see, indisputable. It grew under the moon and under the sun, it put out branches and threw out leaves with an extravagance that looked to Becky like sheer joy at being alive. And it was going to ramp all over the graveyard, she could see that, so it certainly had no respect for the dead.

In short, it was a friend. And because she could not speak to it, or smile, or shake hands, or make any of the ordinary signs of friendship, she stretched out a hand and touched it, for the first time. For a moment she was aware of its coolness and strength, then she actually gave it a brief, awkward shake, and let it go abruptly. A little magic at a time was enough to begin with.

'. . . to get back,' came Finch's voice, 'and see about them trees in your mother's garden.'

A bargain had been sealed, and he had not even noticed.

Chapter Eight

'Going to leave it, is he?' said Jason. 'Hasn't he heard of magic?'

'Nobody said anything about magic,' Becky replied. 'Even if I had, he wouldn't have believed it.'

She felt irritated with Jason, for no fault of his own. Finch had gone round to the Big House to tell Mrs Harper about the Bongleweed. With any luck, she would make him take off his boots and then take him into the sitting-room. She had an objection to 'holding conversations on the kitchen doorstep'.

Else was still out, so the coast was clear. Becky could have lifted down the Bubble Boy and watched the whole thing. She was torn between foregoing this delicious pleasure, and letting Jason into the secret of the spyhole. She decided to test him out.

'D'you like the Harpers?' she asked carelessly. 'D'you like Mrs Harper?'

'Aunt Delia?' He shrugged. 'She's all right. Fussy, you know. Bit of a fogey. When I've been

70

here a bit, I might do something about shaking her up.'

'You'll be lucky,' Becky told him, nonetheless pleased with the answer. Then 'But after all, she is a relation of yours, isn't she?'

'What's in a word?' said Jason.

'You don't believe in all that stuff about blood being thicker than water, then?' she pressed.

'Well, it is, isn't it? Stands to sense. You don't get *water* clotting. Blood does. Hey, that's good. Aunt Delia is a blood relation—in other words, a bit of a clot. Get it?'

He was being clever again, Becky realized, but again she was pleased. She gave him a third and last question (since all the tests and trials she had ever read about seemed to go in threes).

'If you had to choose between the Bongleweed and Mrs Harper, which would you choose?'

'The weed.' Jason's reply was prompt, brief, and decisive.

'Come on,' she said. 'I want to show you something. But first, you've got to swear.'

'Bloody hell,' said Jason obligingly.

Becky giggled.

'Swear *properly*, I mean.'

'Bloody, blasted, b——'

'Jason!' she wailed.

In the end, he did swear. He crossed his heart,

hoped to die and went through the whole elaborate ritual of promise-keeping.

'There!' he said, when it was all over. 'Satisfied? I'll shrivel up and drop dead if I so much as say a word now. So what's the secret? It'd better be good.'

'It is good,' she told him. 'Follow me.'

They went through the arch leading from Pew into the work gardens, up the slabbed path to the back door and into the shadowy, loudly ticking kitchen.

'Gosh,' Jason said, looking round. 'It's small.'

'Now look,' Becky said. 'From now on, you haven't got to say a word. If you make so much as a sound, you'll ruin the whole thing.'

He stared.

'For ever more,' she added, aware for the first time of the enormity of what she was doing. Her marvellous private peepshow hung now on Jason's silence.

'We're going in the parlour,' she told him, '*lounge*, I mean. And every single little tiny sound can be heard next door.'

His eyes widened.

'In your Aunt Delia's sitting-room,' she said.

She opened the door. The parlour was dimmer still, its silence deeper. It was as if the very air had settled into silence through long habit, disturbed nowadays only by Else's cautious dusting of her ornaments and shaking of cushions.

'Gosh,' began Jason, and his voice exploded into the room, so that Becky turned and gave him a violent push back into the passage, pulling the door to with the other hand.

'Shut up!' she hissed. 'Didn't you *hear* what I said?'

'Sorry. I forgot.'

'Well *don't* forget!' she flashed. 'You don't seem to *realize*. You haven't even got to *sneeze*. Now can you keep quiet, or can't you?'

'Keep your hair on. I'll keep quiet.'

'Well mind you do. Now *shut up*.'

She opened the door again and sensed with relief that the silence had settled again. Next door, all was quiet. All the same she tiptoed over to the fireside chair, stood on it, and carefully lifted down the solemnly staring Bubble Boy. As she placed it against the chair she caught sight of Jason. He was talking with his face now—face and hands. He raised his eyebrows up into his hair, popped his eyes, pointed to the picture, mouthed words. Becky shook her head at him severely, and in the same moment heard Mrs Harper's voice.

She turned and put her eye to the spyhole in time to catch a glimpse of Mrs Harper's carefully permed grey hair, which disappeared almost instantly to give place to a pair of brown-socked feet and trouser-bottoms. Finch's. The feet stood there in the doorway.

'Come along in, Finch,' came Mrs Harper's voice. 'You can sit here.'

She was offering him, Becky guessed, the old chair, the one that needed recovering. If it ever *were* covered, she supposed that Finch would in future have to stand there throughout his interviews with the Harpers, cut off from comfort by the dusty state of his trousers.

The brown socks moved, and the stage was set. Unfortunately, from Becky's point of view it was an empty one. She took her eye away from the hole, put her finger to her lips to remind Jason, and settled down to listen.

'Now, Finch,' said Mrs Harper. 'What is it?'

There was a long pause. (All conversations with Finch included long pauses.)

'It's a matter to do with the plants, Mrs Harper!'

'With the plants? Did you say plants?'

There was another pause, and then Finch's voice, very loud—he had evidently just remembered that Mrs Harper was slightly deaf.

'*Plants*, ma'am.'

'All right, Finch. There is no need to shout. I heard you perfectly well the first time. It's simply that I am surprised that you should wish to consult me about such matters.'

'I'm sorry,' said Finch. 'I'm very sorry. But it's urgent. It's urgent.'

'Urgent?' she echoed.

'Urgent. You might say *very* urgent.'

'But, Finch,' said Mrs Harper, 'did the doctor not leave instructions that you should telephone Doctor . . . Doctor . . . what's his name? That very tall man with a large head and that irritating cough. Most irritating. Pure affectation, I should say.'

'Doctor Ainger,' said Finch. 'I rung him.'

'Rang him,' said Mrs Harper. 'And what did he advise?'

'Nothing.'

'Nothing?'

'Nothing. Gone away. Gone to India. Back in a month. Gone away.'

There was another pause. Jason and Becky, crouched together in the corner, made elaborate faces at one another and Becky put a hand over her mouth to stifle a giggle.

'Very well, Finch.' Becky could imagine her now, sitting bolt upright in her chair, bracing herself to make a botanical decision. 'Now what is the problem?'

The pause that followed was so long that it was hard to believe that anybody was still there, and Becky actually put her eye to the spyhole again. Though she could perfectly well understand her father's difficulty. How did you begin to explain to a person like Mrs Harper that a South American Bongleweed was rampant in Pew, that magic had been let loose? For Finch, to whom even a remark about the weather was an effort, explanation must be a near impossibility.

At last Finch's voice came, from the wings.

'There is a plant that is overgrowing. It is growing at a fast rate such as I've not seen ever before.'

'And is that bad?' enquired Mrs Harper. 'Is it an important one? One of the doctor's crosses?'

'I daresay it's a cross, all right,' agreed Finch. 'Ain't even got a name, so far as I know. But it ain't one of the doctor's. It's from seed a gentleman give him at that Conference in January.'

'Ah, well.' Mrs Harper sounded relieved. 'There's nothing strange in that, as far as I can see. Possibly it is a species that *makes* fast growth, Finch.'

Hark at her, Becky thought, telling Dad his job.

'When I say the word fast, Mrs Harper,' came Finch's voice, 'I mean . . . I mean . . . ' pause—'*fast.*'

'I'm sure you do, Finch. But what am I to say? If this is a fast-growing plant, then we must let nature take its course.'

'It ain't nature.' Finch's voice was dogged now. 'It ain't nature.'

'Then what on earth *is* it?' Mrs Harper's voice was irritable.

'It ain't nature,' repeated Finch. These were evidently the only words he could find to fit the situation. After all, Becky thought, nobody knew better than Finch what nature *was*, so it was reasonable that he should recognize what *wasn't*, when he saw it. Further than that he could not go.

'Now, Finch,' said Mrs Harper briskly, 'we must have no more of this nonsense. The doctor has every confidence in you, and has left you countless times in charge of things here in Pew. You must simply use your own discretion. Your own initiative.'

Finch made one last desperate effort.

'If you could just come and have a look, Mrs Harper . . .'

'Where is this extraordinary plant?'

'It's on the compost heap. Least, it was last time I looked.'

'Now *whatever* do you mean by that?'

'Last time I looked, it was on the compost heap. It was over the railings and into the graveyard.'

And could be up the tower by now! thought Becky with a rush of excitement. Up the tower and strangling the weathercock! Oh Glory, Mrs H., if you only knew!

'I have no idea what you are talking about,

Finch,' came Mrs Harper's voice. 'But one thing is perfectly clear. The doctor would plant nothing that he valued on the—compost heap. And so I shall give you some advice. My advice is to go straight out there, and dig it up.'

'Yes, ma'am,' said Finch mechanically. 'That's what I thought. Dig it up. Or spray it.'

'I leave the technicalities entirely to you, Finch,' said Mrs Harper. 'I'm sure you know how to cope with the situation far better than I.'

There was the scrape of a chair on the parquet and swiftly Becky put her eye to the spyhole again. The brown socks were in view, neatly, side by side, as if the wearer were standing to attention.

'Thank you. Thank you very much, Mrs Harper,' they said.

'Not at all, Finch. I'm always available in an emergency, as you know. Though I do not think you need ever feel that you must consult me again about a . . . about a *weed*, Finch.'

'No, Mrs Harper. Thank you, Mrs Harper.'

The brown socks turned about and the interview was at an end. A moment later there was a glimpse of permed grey hair, then a tweed skirt, then brogue shoes. The sitting-room door closed—or, from Becky's point of view, the curtain dropped.

'There!' she whispered, turning to Jason. '*Now* do you see?'

For answer, he pushed her aside and put his own eye to the spyhole. After a time he took it away again.

'What a spying little wretch you are,' he said.

Chapter Nine

Finch, as Becky had hoped, did not go straight to the graveyard to launch an attack on the Bongleweed. With his unerring sense of priorities he first set about the task of clearing Else's garden before she returned from Selling.

'And it'll take him all day, just about,' Becky told Jason gleefully. 'And any time that's left, he'll have to do his rounds in Pew. Keep an eye on the under-gardeners, and all that.'

'So the Bongleweed'll have another day to grow in,' said Jason.

'And another night,' she reminded him. 'First *grew* under the moon, remember. Oh, Jason, I keep believing it and *not* believing it. I keep wanting to go and see if it's still there. I mean, what if it wasn't really there, and only a figment of imagination?'

'You can't have figments of *two* people's imaginations,' said Jason. 'I mean three—no, four—your mother's seen it as well.'

'I bet you can,' she said. 'I bet you can have figments of *thousands* of people's imaginations.'

'At the rate that Bongleweed's growing,' Jason said, 'it'll soon be a figment of all *England's* imaginations.'

'Sshhh!'

They were standing just outside the kitchen door, in the moving emblems of sun and shadow made by an apple tree old as the house itself. The wind was shimmering the whole garden and in the distance, over the wall and somewhere in the green hidey-hole of Pew itself, a cuckoo called.

'Cuckoo! Cuckoo!'

Becky felt a deep stir in every inch of her flesh, the inexplicable sense of miracle that came each time she heard the cuckoo. It seemed to her so private and elusive a bird that she always thought of it as shadowless, and its call as an echo. Never once had she seen it, and she had no wish to. And no one in the world had ever seen a cuckoo's nest. There was no such thing—and that in itself seemed to bear out her theory. Fleetingly she thought:

The cuckoo's a figment of the imagination!

Aloud, she said:

'Two more months of cuckoos. Every day, now!'

'Let's go and see what your father's up to,' said Jason, and they went right under the blowing apple blossom and round the corner of the house and saw Finch.

He was doing nothing—or at least, nothing visible. He stood, boots astride, one hand resting on a longhandled axe, staring up at the Bongleweed. He was staring—not *looking*, and probably not even seeing at all. He was thinking, and had been thinking, so Becky guessed, for ten minutes at least.

And for every minute he's thinking, she thought, it's growing another inch. If he stands there thinking much longer, he'll end up with it wrapped *round* him!

'Hello, Dad,' she said. 'Going to chop it, are you?'

'I don't rightly know, Becky,' he answered at length. 'I can't seem to come round to knowing what the right answer is. If it wasn't for your mother, I should feel like waiting a bit. See what happens.'

Finch, she knew, hated to fell. He winced at every stroke of the axe, as if he were feeling the pain of it himself.

'Seems a pity, Mr Finch,' said Jason. 'To chop a phenomenon.'

Clearly Finch did not even hear him. Thinking, for him, involved the temporary shutting off of all his other faculties. He thought, as he did everything else, thoroughly.

Becky, realizing that any attempts at conversation would be useless, turned her attention to the Bongleweed.

We could only've left one or two, she thought with awe, and look at it!

It had taken over Else's garden entirely.

'No wonder she went mad.'

Her gaze travelled from the thick, succulent stems up past the first waving tendrils to the brilliantly green and shaking mass of leaves above, and—

'Dad!' she shrieked. 'Dad!'

Finch jerked violently, came to as a sleepwalker might, momentarily dazed.

'Look! Look there!'

Finch and Jason followed the direction of her pointing finger.

'Buds!' cried Jason. 'And there! Look—all over! It's covered in them!'

It was. The Bongleweed was breaking into prodigal bud with the same effortless speed and ease as it had first soared skyward, north, south, east, and westward, under the moon.

'Oh!' Becky gasped. 'And it's beautiful!'

The buds were of a deep apricot, almost like those of magnolia only larger—twice as large— three times. They were tightly furled and yet had an extraordinary sheen and delicacy, as if they would open out like umbrellas of sheerest silk.

Finch was shaking his head as if he would never stop. A lifetime's study of the laws of nature was being thrown to the winds under his very eyes.

He groaned then, and Becky guessed that it was a groan of anguish, and helplessness and disbelief and joy—surely joy? No gardener on earth could resist the spectacle of such glorious growth and vigour. The Bongleweed was uncontainable in its urge to spread, climb, put forth.

'But they wasn't there.' It was Finch himself who broke the silence. 'An hour since, they wasn't there!'

'And in another hour, they'll be flowers!' cried Becky, and in the instant of speaking came another realization. The Bongleweed, by breaking into bud, had averted its own doom.

'And there's no need to chop it now! It can stop!'

The others shifted their gaze and looked at her.

'It'll be *flowering* when Mum gets back! And look at them buds—*huge* them flowers'll be—big as dinner plates! Don't you see? There's no need to chop it now!'

Finch, at last, was nodding. He *did* see. Else, with her weakness for even the smallest flower of the most pernicious weed, would forgive the Bongleweed at first sight, take it under her wing and cherish it, fiercely and protectively, against all attack. Once Else got home, the Bongleweed would be chopped over her own dead body.

'I'm going to stop here!' Becky cried. 'I'm going to stop and *see* them buds open out! Let's all! Let's fetch chairs and sit and watch it happen!'

But Finch's head was shaking again. Already he had seen more than he could come to terms with. And even Jason looked dubious.

'I don't think we should,' he said. 'If we did, it might not happen. I think we should go away and leave it in private.'

'But what shall we *do*?' cried Becky in desperation. How to fill an hour when all the time, for a certainty, those enormous buds were visibly and silently unfurling?

'Oh, I shall go and sit with my head in a paper *bag*!'

'Come along, Becky,' Finch told her and, with a last disbelieving shake of his head, led the way back past the house.

'Time will pass,' he added—as if glad to be able to make a statement that *was* irrefutable, some kind of straw to cling to.

It's all very well saying that, thought Becky rebelliously. But there's time and *time*. And this kind of time I just can't bear—I can't!

Chapter Ten

The hour before Else's return, the hour during which the Bongleweed's buds would break forth, did, in fact, pass.

Jason and Becky went into a potting shed and made up for not being able to see the Bongleweed by speculating about what form its flowers would take. Jason favoured an umbrella shape, and thought that although the buds seemed to be of the same shade, the flowers themselves would be all the colours of the rainbow, from yellow to indigo—and striped, even.

Becky herself thought this a little far-fetched, and said so. But Jason pointed out that if anything was far-fetched, then that thing was the Bongleweed, and that he himself would put nothing past it, *nothing*.

Becky was inclined to think that the buds would open into a kind of giant, *giant* sunflower.

'Or moonflower, even,' she added as an after-thought. 'Because sure as eggs that weed first started shooting in the night. *And* whispering. It did, you know, for that was what fetched me out of bed. I heard it. It's as if it was alive.'

'It's alive, all right,' Jason said. 'And kicking.'

'No, *really* alive, I mean, like you and me,' Becky persisted. '*Meaning* something.'

'Magic,' he said briefly. 'You've got to face it. Like that witch in Brum. I bet if she was to see the Bongleweed, she wouldn't turn a hair. Probably her seeds, if we only knew it.'

'But it was a man who gave 'em,' Becky told him. 'A man with whiskers, the doctor said, at a conference.'

'Her in disguise,' suggested Jason. 'Or Mr Crump.'

Becky giggled.

'Now what?' he demanded stiffly.

'I'm sorry. It's just the name. I mean, a witch called Mrs Crump with a husband called Mr Crump . . .'

'It's twelve!' Jason leapt up. 'Come on. Your mother'll be back in five minutes.'

They came out of the potting shed into the sharp April sun and again the cuckoo called and next minute they were past the house and staring up at the Bongleweed.

'Oh!' Becky exclaimed softly at last. 'Oh!'

Till now she had thought of the weed as a rogue,

a rascal, an outsized botanical scallywag. But now she saw that it was beautiful too.

The mere fact that these flowers were flowers at all was amazing enough under the circumstances. But that they should be so outsized, so unrepentantly and wickedly beautiful, was more than even Becky herself had bargained for. Their very colour was flagrant—russet and nasturtium and apricot, depending on whether they were in shadow or sun, half furled or fully opened. In the centre of some she glimpsed dark brown stamens, inches long, antennae. The texture of the petals was such that the flowers seemed to float among the foliage rather than grow out of it, waft, more like moths than blossom. In a way, they hardly seemed to belong to the weed at all—hothouse flowers pinned on to a sturdy, all-seasons perennial.

And more than ever now the weed seemed what Becky had called 'alive' (for want of a better word) because of the perpetual stream of its colours down the wind and the glint of its great leaves.

They were still staring as Else came banging through the gate. She stopped dead, face flushed and bag bulging, and to Becky's startled gaze seemed for an instant to be *herself* an apparition, so odd a figure did she cut beside that fabulous weed. For the blink of an eye, Becky hardly believed in her own mother.

'Oh my good gracious!' said Else, and dropped her bag.

She stood motionless for what seemed a full minute, and again Becky was able to grasp the unspeakable oddity of the tableau. There stood Else, felt-hatted and predictable as sunrise, and there stood—or rather stretched—the Bongleweed, tricky as a fox and twice as beautiful, impossible as snow in August. The church clock, never in a hurry, struck twelve as they stood, and Becky, automatically counting, found herself actually waiting for the thirteenth stroke. It did not come. But the sound, a certain reminder of both time and place, seemed to rouse Else out of her mazed speechlessness.

'Them's those trees!' she cried. 'What are they doing with *flowers* on 'em? Whatever's been going on while I've been gone?'

Her voice was accusing, as if she suspected Becky and Finch of some elaborate hoax, as if she actually thought *them* responsible. She advanced then, her bag forgotten, and stood right beneath the Bongleweed, staring up as if hypnotized at those illuminated flowers, actually putting out a hand and touching—gingerly—one of the great leaves. She snatched it back again immediately.

'Don't sting,' she said, inconsequentially, as though if it *had* stung the whole matter would

have been explained. 'Oh my word, did you ever see such a thing? Whatever on earth is it?'

'It's a weed, Mum,' said Becky craftily, watching her mother's face.

'It never in this world is!' cried Else indignantly. 'I suppose that's your father's idea. It's downright beautiful, that's what it is. It'd knock any of his stuff out there'—with a jerk of her head towards Pew—'into a cocked hat. Weed indeed! I could stand here all day, I declare I could, just looking at it.'

And the way she was standing there, oblivious of the bag of fish, of the time, of anything in the world, it almost seemed as if she might do that very thing.

'What is it?' she said again, half to herself.

'It's the South American Bongleweed, Mum,' Becky said. '*We* grew it, Jason and me, from seed, only day before yesterday.'

'Day before yesterday?' Else whipped round. 'Such rubbish!'

'We did, Mum. Think—it wasn't there yesterday, was it?'

'No more it wasn't,' agreed Else slowly. 'Well, there's a thing.'

'So you see, Mum, it *is* a weed,' Becky went on. 'Must be. There's only a weed'd grow that fast.'

'That's true,' agreed Else mechanically. It was

as if she had already accepted the Bongleweed, size and all, and the sheer impossibility of its being there at all had bypassed her entirely. It was there, it had grown from seed since the day before yesterday, and that was that.

'So Dad thinks it'll have to come down.' Becky pressed her advantage. 'You know what he is about weeds.'

'Come down!' Else half shrieked. 'Come *down*? It never will! *My* garden this is, and I've told him before, *I* decide what's weeds and what isn't. And if that comes down, it'll be over my dead body!'

Becky let out a long-held breath of relief. Finch versus Else, herself, and the Bongleweed itself— the fight was as good as won. In fact, it would hardly be a fight at all. Finch's own inclination to axe the weed had been lukewarm, and in any case, she reflected, he probably believed that it had now stopped growing.

Becky, on the other hand, believed nothing of the kind. The Bongleweed, it seemed obvious, was only just getting into its stride.

'Well!' said Else again, with a final stare. 'I shall have to get on.'

She looked vaguely about, saw the bag, snatched it up, and marched on round the back of the house.

'Phew!' Jason himself was still staring upwards

and the sun flashed full on his spectacles, making him look positively dazzled by disbelief. 'Clever stuff, Becky. *She* won't let him chop it down.'

'I told you. Got a soft spot for weeds. Nearly drives Dad mad sometimes. Come on, Jason.'

He looked at her.

'Where?'

'Compost heap. What'll *that* be like?'

Jason nodded and they began to run, past the house, through the work gardens and at last to the furthest boundary where Pew and the graveyard met at the iron railings. They stopped. Without a word they stood and took it all in.

The scene before them was changed, translated as it might be by frost or snow. Becky blinked to see a kind of fire let loose among sternly towering saints and stone angels with uplifted eyes and praying palms. The green had gently and inexorably parcelled headstones and bound the granite crosses with living rope, imprisoned them. Each sign of death was made null and cancelled out by the unmistakable print of life. Not a slab or a tomb was left to read—not even the great monument of Sir William Crane (Peace Perfect Peace) and his wife Elisabeth (Come Unto Me All Ye That Labour).

The Hannahs and Williams and Sarah Janes late of this parish were slumbering oblivious in a jungle. Sober yews had broken into unlikely bud and in the midst of it all Becky glimpsed the head of an angel, cheeks puffed out, blowing a trumpet—the last trump, she supposed, and well it might be. She had often looked at this particular angel and thought how conscientious he looked, but today he seemed to have his cheeks puffed to positive bursting point, in an all-out, frantic blast of warning against the invading greenery.

Once she had taken in the extravagantly decorated graveyard, Becky became aware of something else out of the ordinary. At first she could not place what it was, stunned out of reason by that incorrigible weed. But as her eyes grew slowly accustomed to shock the rest of her senses returned, and she knew, all in a moment, what it was.

'The birds!' she cried. 'Just hark at them!'

The harmless English thrush and blackbird, robin and wren, were joined in a furious chorus of protest. Laurel and hawthorn, bush and shrub, every familiar leaf and twig had vanished, and along with them half-built nests and accepted territories. She spotted them ranged along the church guttering or perched high on yew, twittering helplessly at the alien weed, homeless, wormless, and with scarcely a landmark left in sight.

'What'll they do?' she cried.

'Get used to it,' Jason said. 'Same as we're

doing. Birds've only got brains the size of a pea. You can't be *that* surprised with a brain that size.'

'True,' agreed Becky, nonetheless dubious. It seemed to her that the Bongleweed was affecting the birds rather more than themselves. 'It's their homes though, isn't it?'

'For all we know,' replied Jason, 'it'll be *our* homes next.'

Becky let out a high, nervous shriek. A sudden picture of her own home cocooned in leaves and giant orchids flashed before her eyes.

'Too late now for selective weed-killer,' she heard herself saying.

'Too late now for anything,' he said. 'Too late—full stop.'

'Ooooh!' Becky gave a slow, delicious shudder.

She stretched out her arms in a vain attempt to embrace the Bongleweed, to demonstrate in a gesture the love she felt for it. At that moment it seemed as if there would never, ever be a dull moment again. If she stayed another minute, she would choke with excitement. So she did not stay. She fled.

Chapter Eleven

Jason had not followed her. Becky stopped, panting, back under the deckling apple boughs, and listened for footsteps. She dropped to the grass. Her mind was racing and yet another part of her was curiously alert and aware. She was conscious that the grass was damp and warm under her spread palms, that the ancient trunk of the apple was not brown, as she had supposed, but grey, ridged and pitted as a lunar landscape and crusted with moss. She felt so aware and yet so beautifully contained in her happiness that it was as if the whole world were spoking out from a central point somewhere deep inside herself—somewhere in her head, she supposed, behind her eyes.

'Beautiful weed,' she murmured. 'O beautiful weed, beautiful pea-green wild and wonderful weed!'

A window was being opened somewhere to her right. She stood up and saw that it was one of the long sashes in Mrs Harper's sitting-room.

If they're both in there, she thought, Mum and Mrs H., they might be talking about the Bongleweed.

Finch, she knew, was far away now in the watery green distances of Pew, marshalling the under-gardeners, caught up in his daily round and the weed, as likely as not, quite forgotten. Days in Pew had patterns for Finch, they rose and fell and went forward greenly and inexorably as tides, and he with them.

She went in, took a biscuit from the barrel as she passed the dresser, and next minute was face to face with the Bubble Boy. She shook her head at him.

'What a spying little wretch I am!' she whispered, and lifted him down. He was a comfort to her, really—his expression never changed. There was never the least hint on his upturned face of criticism or blame.

The only sounds from next door were the unmistakable ones of Else's dusting (things being picked up and put down again) and the occasional crackle of a newspaper. Mrs Harper always found time in the mornings for the newspaper, and Becky guessed that she had spent the first part of the day arranging flowers for her dinner party that evening, and was now making up for lost time.

She hardly *ever* goes for a walk in Pew, Becky

thought. Ah, there's Mum's legs, now. Can't think why she married the doctor in the first place, or him her, for that matter.

This was not the first time she had speculated about this. The only enlightening thought she had so far had on the subject was that the name Delia had reminded the doctor of dahlia, and he had become married to her in a purely absent-minded, botanical kind of way.

'I think that will do now, Elsie,' she heard Mrs Harper say. 'You gave the room a good turnout yesterday—it was just a matter of dusting. Perhaps you had better go off and see to your own meal, so that you can be back here in good time this afternoon.'

'That'll be best, Mrs Harper,' agreed Elsie. 'I'll lay up the table first thing, while the meringues is drying out. Six lovely plaice fillets I got, and I must say it does pay, going in and having a pick over for yourself.'

'Yes, I'm sure it does, Elsie,' said Mrs Harper, and there was another rustle of newspaper.

Rude thing, thought Becky, she's not listening to a word Mum's saying.

'Oooh, and I must just tell you, Mrs Harper,' came Else's voice, just as her feet became visible in the doorway. 'I've got the most *beautiful* tree things growing in our garden round the front. Beautiful.

Finch says it's a weed, but I'm sure it's no such thing. Beautiful!'

'Really, Else? Lovely . . .'

'And the rummest thing, you'd never believe! Grown from seed our Becky and your Jason put in only day before yesterday. And the size of it! And the flowers—big as your own head and handsome—fair *handsome*!'

The feet *fidgeted* with emotion.

'Oh, *Mum*!' cried Becky silently. 'Shut up, do!'

If Mrs Harper were to go outside and see for herself what was afoot, likely as not she would set the whole Pew army of gardeners on to the Bongleweed. But such fears were groundless.

'Lovely . . .' murmured Mrs Harper. 'I must take a look some time, when I'm passing . . .'

'Well, if that'll be all, Mrs Harper?'

'Thank you, Elsie, that will be all, for now.'

The door shut. Becky placed the Bubble Boy back on his nail and shook her head at him. It seemed quite likely that *he* had more idea of what was going on than Mrs Harper had—head in the newspaper like an ostrich.

'S all right knowing what's going on in the world, she thought, and then not knowing what's going on on your own *doorstep*.

She met Else by the back door, hands halfway up towards unpinning her hat.

'C'm'on, Mum,' she said, tugging at her arm. 'Let's go and have another look at it.'

Else hesitated, then dropped her hands.

'Just for a minute, then,' she agreed. 'But I'm in a dash, mind, and no time for standing about while the grass grows under my feet.'

Becky giggled.

'It's not the grass,' she said, but Else was already off ahead of her, and had not heard. By the corner of the house she stood, still wearing her hat and pinafore, and waved her hands in a gesture of helpless admiration.

'Oh I declare!' she cried. 'It's growed since I last saw it, I swear it has!'

'Oh it will have, Mum,' Becky assured her. 'Pity you've not got time to fetch a chair and sit here watching. You'd *see* it grow then, you really would. Them buds, they turn into flowers in under an hour.'

'I never!' Else's face was turned upward in rapt contemplation. 'Just like on them films, on the television. You remember, Becky, that one where we saw that rose opening up—didn't take two minutes, let alone an hour. But I never thought to have one like it in my own garden!'

Again Becky saw that the absolute impossibility of the Bongleweed had escaped her mother entirely.

''Course,' Else was saying, 'it's done for my sweet william, you can see that. But there you are. What did you say its name was, Becky?'

'The Bongleweed, Mum. The South American Bongleweed.'

'Mmmmmmm.' The flowers were brimful with sunlight, suffused with it so that each individual blossom seemed itself to be a source of faint, glowing light. The heads were alive, they sniffed the wind like pale, fluorescent foxes.

'Not a very *pretty* name. But what's a name? You've got to take things as you find 'em, and never mind names. T'ain't as if they're things you *choose*.'

I did, thought Becky, and wondered fleetingly whether she had chosen wrongly, and even whether if she had picked a different name, the *weed* would have been different. The thought took her by surprise. What if she, by naming the weed, had created it, so to speak?

Well, and what if I did? she thought. Couldn't have made a better job of it, *whatever* I'd called it.

And the thought stayed with her, so that now her gaze at the Bongleweed was proprietary as well as loving, the kind of look a mother might give her new baby. Admittedly the Bongleweed was not *like* a baby, except in the sense of having been newly born. Already it had a reckless independence, a will of its own. It was a hooligan. It would go its own way, no matter what, and everything and everyone whose path it crossed (or even blocked) would be changed because of it.

Within half an hour the Finches were sitting down to their meal—a makeshift one, to leave Else's real skills as cook free for the preparation of Mrs Harper's dinner. For once, however, Becky did not sulk as she eyed the cold meat and salad which always seemed to her to be an insult—a non-meal if ever there was one.

'What a mercy you didn't go chopping down my trees,' Else told Finch, popping a couple of tomatoes on to his plate.

Her trees indeed! Becky thought, though she could see that Else's adoption of the weed was by no means a bad thing.

'Prettiest things I ever saw—and the *size*! And if you'd've seen the way the sun was shining through them petals!'

Finch shook his head.

'Now don't you go getting yourself too set on it, Else,' he said. 'There's nothing certain, yet.'

'There's one thing certain!' said Else, spiritedly slicing cucumber on to Becky's plate.

Finch picked up his knife and fork without replying.

'There's one thing certain!' repeated Else aggressively. 'Them trees is stopping.'

'There's more to it than that, Else,' he said. 'There's more like it. In the graveyard.'

'In the *graveyard*?'

'Ramping mad,' affirmed Finch. 'Not hardly a tombstone left in sight, last time I looked. I'm tom in half by it all, and that's a fact.'

The others looked at him surprised by the revelation of what were, for Finch, dramatic feelings.

'There's part of me,' he went on, 'says that's a weed. Not a doubt of it. A weed.'

'Oh, I knew *that* was what you'd say!' cried Else.

'And then there's this other part that says this is unusual. This is very unusual.'

'*I've* never seen its like,' agreed Else.

'It's a mystery,' said Finch. 'Them self same seeds we planted in the tropical, what did they do?'

There was a pause.

'Well, what did they?' prompted Else.

'Shot up,' he said. 'Then fell down.'

Ring a ring o' roses, Becky found herself thinking. A pocket full o' posies. Atishoo, Atishoo! We all fall down.

'Too hot for them,' said Else sensibly. 'That'd be it. I'd fall flat on *my* face if I was to be in there more'n half an hour.'

104

Finch was looking at her now with something like respect.

'That's just what I've come round to thinking myself,' he said. 'Exact. Too hot.'

'Well, there we are, then!' cried Else. 'It'll go a treat, round the front there. And just got put in right for the growing weather.'

Finch paled, then put down his knife and fork.

'I shall have to think,' he muttered. 'I shall have to think,' and stood up.

'Now where're you going?' demanded Else.

For answer Finch shook his head, took his cap from its nail, and went out.

'Well!'

Else, Becky could see, was more taken aback by Finch's untoward behaviour than she had been by the sight of the Bongleweed itself. Finch, who had always been an open book to her, was himself translated, so to speak.

'It was what you said about growing weather that upset him, Mum,' said Becky. 'I think you ought to go down and look at the graveyard.'

'I shall do no such thing!' returned Else with asperity. 'You get on with your dinner, Becky, and keep out of it! Such a fuss!'

They ate in silence while the clock ticked.

Every tick an inch, Becky thought. Every tock *another* inch.

The shaft of sunlight that lay across her plate disappeared all at once.

'Clouding over,' Else remarked. 'April shower, next thing. What I said—growing weather.'

Then it'll be tick two inches, tock two inches, thought Becky. Don't she *realize*?

'And don't you go running off with that boy this afternoon and him nowhere to be found when he's wanted,' said Else. 'He's to have dinner with the company, and to have a bath first, Mrs H. says.'

'Who else is coming?' asked Becky. The after-dinner conversation in the sitting-room might be interesting.

'Vicar and his wife and the Doctor Stoneses. Now here's your rice pudding, Becky, and mind the dish, it's hot.' She was pinning on her hat now. 'You can clear away and wash up, and tea'll be at five sharp.' She opened the door. 'And mind what I said about that boy.'

The door closed. The clock came back into its own again, and the room darkened. The dimmer it grew, the louder the clock seemed to tick. Becky, cautiously scooping hot rice from the edge of the dish and counting ten before she put it gingerly to her mouth, became aware of another, lighter ticking—a kind of counterpoint.

She looked up. Rain was slanting on to the

window, breaking as it touched the glass and blurring the apple tree into a green waterfall. She put down her spoon and wandered out, under the tree and round the house, in a kind of dream. She stood and stared upward at the Bongleweed and the rain splashed on to her face and went into her eyes, making her blink.

The giant moth-foxes, struck by the heavy drops, were flapping against the dark sky. Becky's vision was filled by the long silvery needles of rain and the restlessly tossed greenery. And beyond the pattering was another sound, a faint hissing—or sucking?—as if the weed were drinking greedily, taking its fill like a thirsty beast.

'Oh, weed,' she whispered, 'you *are* alive. But don't come too close, will you?'

Only a bare two yards now lay between the ranging Bongleweed and her own front door. She saw a sudden picture of herself down on a darkening beach, building a castle of sand and pebbles against the incoming tide. She could see the streaked sky and the slipping walls and feel the inrush of icy water about her ankles and the surge of a momentarily real panic.

There's *no* wall high enough to keep it out, she thought. And she stood there, heedlessly drenched, while the rain fed life into the Bongleweed, and felt, for the first time, afraid.

Chapter Twelve

'. . . an absolute treasure.'

Black shiny shoes and the bottom half of a long mauve frock came into view.

That's Mum she's talking about, thought Becky, sure as eggs.

There followed a procession of feet and frocks, feet and trousers. Jason's came last, easily recognizable though strangely neat and formal. The feet were followed by faces—more glimpses—the vicar and Mrs Waters, Dr and Mrs Stone. Then Jason, scowling at their backs.

Becky, who had earlier been envious of Jason's share of Else's dinner (cucumber soup, plaice, meringues sandwiched with cream and swimming in hot orange chocolate sauce) now felt herself with relish to be in the superior position.

She had hardly expected the company to launch straight into a conversation about the Bongleweed, and was therefore not surprised when the first subject up for discussion was holidays abroad. The dullness of this was more than compensated for, however, by the perfectly delightful coincidence that Jason's face was in full view through the spyhole. It wore an expression of such profound and unconcealed boredom that Becky wondered whether he thought perhaps he was invisible behind his spectacles (an illusion she sometimes had herself when she wore sunglasses).

'And have you been abroad, Jeremy?'

It was the Reverend Mr Waters speaking, in his best visiting manner.

There was a silence.

'Jason!' came the black patent shoes and mauve frock fractionally representing Mrs Harper.

'Oh, me! Sorry!'

He had not even heard the Reverend Mr Waters, and so Becky was cheated of what would have been a considerable scowl. Jason, she knew, was proud of his name. 'It's classical,' he had told her. 'Jason and the Golden Fleece, and all that. A hero.'

And Jeremy, Becky felt certain, was not the name of a hero. The only other hero's name she could think of offhand was Hereward, which, with or without 'the Wake', was not the name of anyone she had ever been introduced to.

Her wandering attention was caught again, this time by the rattle of cups and her mother's voice.

'Coffee, Mrs Harper.'

'Ah, thank you, Elsie.'

Else's feet went behind Jason's head and the door closed.

'Now if I pour, perhaps you'll hand round, Jason. Brandy, everyone?'

There were polite murmurs of assent and Jason's whole person disappeared. Becky, feeling the beginnings of the headache that prolonged squinting through the spyhole usually produced, sank back into the chair and curled up.

Inevitably, her thoughts went straight back to the Bongleweed.

Say and if it *is* a weed, she thought, only a weed such as there's never been before, not in the whole history of the whole world? What then?

She remembered Finch's words:

'If every gardener was to lay down his spade tomorrow, there'd be nothing but buttercups and chickweed from John o' Groats to Lands End in a twelvemonth.'

Had he *meant* it? He had, she decided, after brief thought. Finch was not the man to go wasting words on things he did *not* mean.

In that case, she reflected, he was going to have to look sharp with his selective weed-killer.

Not that that'd harm a hair of its head, and better not! she thought passionately, suddenly seeing the Bongleweed again in her mind's eye, with its fiery flowers that she could think of mysteriously as moths and foxes at one and the same time. She was convinced that nothing Finch or Doctor Harper or even a hundred Doctor Harpers could do would stop the Bongleweed now. It was *there*, still out there in the dark at this very moment, breathing and growing, while the coffee cups clattered and the curtains were drawn and nothing would ever be the same again.

She tried, for the first time, to dare to imagine how it would all end.

If it actually grew and grew and grew and grew, she thought. Then what?

The idea was beyond words, so she tried to see it in pictures, and first of all she saw the Bongleweed up on the roof of their own house, thatching it green and putting flower flames on the chimney pots, shuttering the windows, roping the doors. (Or even coming *in* through the door, if it happened to be open—she almost squealed aloud at the thought—climbing over chairs and tables and up the stairs while Else did valiant battle with broom and kitchen knife.)

Once she had formed a clear picture of this, it was an easy step to see the whole village cocooned, the sky shut out and the people chopping narrow lanes through the jungle, tunnels from house to house so that they could go and sit in one another's

greenish-lit kitchens and wonder where it would all end, and when the fire brigade would arrive and get them out.

I suppose it *would* be the fire brigade's job, she thought. Like if you get your head stuck in the iron railings. You dial 999 and they send the fire brigade.

But the telephone wires? Surely the Bongleweed would run along them at the speed of light, throwing out those thick branches and cucumbery leaves until they snapped under the sheer weight of greenery? The Bongleweed went north, south, east, west, and skyward—it would make for Brum to the north and London to the south. The quickest way, she knew, would be the M1, and she could see it, quite clearly, the long green length of the motorway, silent now, with warning lights flashing non-stop somewhere deep under, and now and again the plaintive, muffled hooting of a trapped motorist . . .

A high-pitched giggle broke into her reverie. It would be Mrs Stone, who giggled at everything. Becky had heard Else say many times that there was no one else she knew who could get squiffy so quick. The giggle was followed by a pause, and then a cough—the one with which the Reverend Mr Waters always prefaced his sermons. Alarmed, Becky hoped that he had not forgotten it was only Saturday yet.

'It hardly seems either the time or place to mention this, Delia,' he mentioned nonetheless, 'but there is just a little matter I was going to draw your attention to, and I suppose I may as well mention it now.'

Becky held her breath.

'It's the graveyard. There seems to be some kind of undergrowth—one might almost say *over*growth—that has covered over the graveyard in the most remarkable way. And as it does seem to originate on your own side of the railings, I wondered whether you might perhaps ask Finch to take it in hand.'

'I believe Finch already has it in hand, Henry,' said the mauve frock. 'He spoke to me about it this very morning, and I advised him to uproot it immediately. I think you will find it has already gone. And I *do* apologize, of course.' A light laugh. 'We hardly go in for weeds at Pew, as you know!'

The vicar coughed again.

'It's good to know you are aware of the problem,' he said, 'but I'm afraid there must have been some misunderstanding on Finch's part. I saw the plant this morning, and I saw it again later in the day. And the growth it had made was really quite extraordinary. And stranger still, it has come into flower. I'm bound to say that it is a most unusual plant, and really of very great beauty. One would almost hesitate to call it a weed at all. But it does represent a very real problem.'

'I've seen it myself, Delia,' put in Mrs Waters, helping him out. 'And really, the entire graveyard is covered in it, on the Pew side of the church.'

'In itself, of course, it's no great matter,' he went on, 'it's simply that it does cover the *graves*, and one has to consider the feelings of the relatives of the deceased.'

'It does all sound queer!' cried Mrs Stone, invisible. 'All over the graveyard, you say, just like that? It wasn't there last week, dear, as you'll remember we came through that side gate for a drink here, after morning service.'

'Don't recollect seeing anything myself,' said Dr Stone, 'but then I'm not altogether at my best on a Sunday morning.'

There was a silence, interrupted only by a particularly painful cough from the vicar.

'Why don't we all go and *look*?' cried Mrs Stone girlishly, and there was a scraping noise that suggested that she had already leapt up from her chair in readiness to do that very thing.

'Now?' intoned the Reverend Mr Waters.

'Now! This very minute! Oh do let's! There's a lovely moon, and it would be such fun! Do say yes, Delia!'

She *is* squiffy, thought Becky, and saw Jason's face, back on stage again, deadpan as he could manage.

'Not a bad evening for a stroll,' agreed her husband. 'Breath of fresh air would do no harm.'

Do *her* no harm, he means, thought Becky. O sweet mystery of life, they're never going to!

But they were. After a few more urgings and protests and a general scuffle of chairs, the entire party rose and left the room in search of coats and wraps.

Becky stuck the Bubble Boy back lopsided and ran for her anorak.

Good job Dad's out, she thought. He was playing darts, as he always did on a Saturday night. He had to do *something* with his hands, even in his time off.

Quietly she opened the back door and stepped out. A moment's listening assured her that the others had not yet come out. She wondered momentarily whether to go down there ahead of them and conceal herself somewhere near the iron railings to wait for them. But she dared not. She even admitted to herself that she dared not. She shivered.

' 'Tis cold,' she told herself, unwilling to admit, too, that her gooseberry arms were anything to do with fright.

The moon was round and white and very high, hanging over Pew like a giant circular Chinese lantern, and transforming all that April green to a mysteriously reshaped landscape in black and silver. The wind had dropped and she heard only a papery flap of damp leaves here and there—no whispering, hushing, guessing . . .

They were coming. Mrs Stone's high giggle floated over the dividing wall, supernaturally clear, as if the moonlight made the air echo, as frost did.

By the time they came through the arched wrought-iron gate, the party had fallen silent. Seen

116

from a little distance, with the misty lawns stretching behind them crowned by the glass pinnacle among the trees, they suddenly seemed more than human. They were like lords and ladies stepping out of a fairy tale. The moonlight silvered their outlines and the long frocks of the ladies swept the gravel with a faint shushing. Even Jason, a small figure in the rear, was made oddly mysterious and shadowy by his silence and pallor.

Now they were passing along a gravelled path edged with box, and more than ever they took on an unreal, floating quality, seeming as they did to glide, only head and shoulders visible now above the hedge, in slow procession, grave and silent.

Becky, staring entranced, almost forgot to follow. Then she ducked and ran forward, and as soon as the party took a right-hand turn, started herself down the path, taking care to keep her own head low. When at last they halted, Becky was able to slip swiftly forward and hide behind a laurel only a few yards away. But it was not at them that she was looking.

She looked, as they did, at the scene beyond the now submerged railings. The graveyard lay in chill flower under the moon. Among the faintly stirring leaves the flowers, drained of colour, were no longer foxy but gone into a dream and become moths again, grey and ghostly, riding the misty

air. The tower of the church rose behind and the weed was steadily climbing it, heavenbent—moonbent. Becky glimpsed the head of the lone trumpet-playing angel, his stone face hollowed and anguished, stiff lips pursed as he soundlessly blew what was, for him, the last trump.

Not a word did the little party of onlookers say. Each, like Becky, was lost in his own imaginings. They shared the same vision, their eyes were all set on the same sight, but there was nothing they could say to one another. It was as if each stood separate and solitary in the limitless acres of the moonlight and faced a solitary dream.

When at last they had seen enough they turned as though by silent consent and began to walk away. They passed within a few feet of the laurel, moving blindly, with rapt, moon-bleached features, like sleepwalkers. The women's frocks, gone lavender and grey, rustled as they went by. Becky followed, and felt the strong, invisible presence of the Bongleweed over her shoulder. Ahead were the lighted windows of the house and soon they would be out of the dark again and into the artificial light, behind drawn curtains. Safe.

Chapter Thirteen

When she woke next morning Becky's thoughts went straight back to the night before. She lay remembering how she had seen the weed in the moonlight and how the others had stood there too, dumbstruck.

When she had got back to the house it had been to find Finch already there, just come in and making himself a cup of tea. Mazed as she was, she was glad of his own silence. Then, at a distance, she had heard the others come back in next door. The sitting-room door must have opened soon after, because there were loud voices, all talking at once, and laughter.

'Listen to them!' she cried inwardly, and felt contempt for them, and disgust. 'How could they?'

They had walked under the moon and seen a miracle only a few minutes since, and now they were back inside and already making a joke of it—a *nothing*, as if it had not mattered. They had stood and seen that weed in all its chill splendour and been struck by wonder, held so fixed by it that it had seemed as if they would never wake again. And already they had forgotten.

She strained at first to hear what they were saying, but gave up.

I can guess, she thought bitterly. Stupid lot! Stupid!

'Cup of tea, Becky?' It was Finch, and having to answer, to break the silence, broke the spell too, and she was suddenly flooded with a sense of the ordinariness of things.

'Yes please, Dad,' she said aloud, and then, to herself, 'But *I* ain't forgotten, not me. It's still *out* there, and they can't stop it. It's there, and laughing their silly heads off don't change that!'

She and Finch sat opposite one another at the table and sipped at their tea. She found herself aware of her father's fingers, thick and blunt-tipped, curled about his steaming mug.

Them's the fingers'll chop that weed, tomorrow, she thought. Sure as eggs, now, she'll make him chop it.

And if Finch were to do it, she would not forgive him.

'Dad!' she cried suddenly. 'Dad!'

He looked up, surprised out of his own thoughts.

'Go out there, Dad, now, go and look!'

He did not answer.

'Listen, I've been—they've all been. Just now—

down to the churchyard. And they've seen it—
we all saw it. And it's magic, real magic, like
Jason said. You'd never believe . . .'

Finch was nodding slowly now.

'Hark at them, Dad, next door! They've seen it
now, and they don't like it. They don't *want* it
here, Dad, and she'll make you chop it. But, Dad,
go and look, will you? Just *look*!'

Again he nodded.

'Now?' she cried. 'Will you?'

For answer he pushed away the mug and stood up.

'You get off to bed, Becky!' was all he said.
'Your mother'll be back.'

He took his cap from the nail and went out.
Becky burst into tears and went upstairs. She was
still weeping softly as she lay in bed and felt the
pillow damp and cold beneath her cheek. Very
faintly now she could hear their voices still next
door, arguing excitedly, laughing.

But Dad's down there, she thought drowsily.
He's gone to see for himself . . .

Finch, too, was to stand alone and try to come
to terms with the impossible. He was down there
now in the quiet garden, he and that stoical
trumpet-playing angel, and the moonstruck moths
of the Bongleweed.

Now, as she lay there, a bell began to ring on one

122

steady, regular note. She sprang up. It must be nearly half past nine, time for the service. She had overslept. Hastily she dressed, then drew back the curtains.

'Oh!' she gasped.

She saw a windowful of foxes in a cucumber green lair. Right against the glass they nuzzled.

Down the stairs she went, two at a time in painful, jarring strides.

Finch and Else sat opposite one another at the kitchen table, a pot of tea between them.

'So you're up,' commented Else. She got up and went to the stove. 'Such goings on. Bed at eight tonight, my girl.'

'But, Mum, Dad, have you seen it?'

'That we have.' Else was tossing rashers into the frying pan. 'Your father's been up since six.'

Finch's face wore an unusual pallor, and looked strained and weary as if he had been up all night, let alone since six.

'Did you see it, Dad?' she whispered, under cover of the sizzling fat and the noisy spurting of water into the kettle. He looked at her and nodded, with a brief attempt at a smile.

'That Mrs Stone,' opined Else loudly, 'wants her head examining. Married to a doctor, and you'd think he'd see it for himself. But then folk never do see what's right under their own noses.'

She sawed off a thick slice of bread with unaccustomed vigour.

'When you're out in that kitchen,' she went on, 'you *hear* folks when they're talking their heads off like they was last night. I'm not a one for listening in on other people's business as well you know, Becky and Finch.'

They did know. No one could have been more punctilious than Else about the instant evacuation of the parlour, whenever the Harpers were on the other side of the partition.

'But there's times it can't be helped, and if you've ears, you've got to hear. And when I think of it . . .'

She cracked an egg into the frying pan.

'I can't see out of my window,' Becky said. 'It's like living in a tree.'

Else was turning the fried bread and bacon on to a plate now. A swift scooping of fat in the pan, and the egg followed. She put the plate in front of Becky, then sat down again herself and began to pour tea all round.

'I shan't ever forget that,' she said. 'Downright beautiful it was, enough to make you weep. It was as if you was standing there wide awake looking to the inside of a dream you was having. Dreaming inside out. I don't know. But I shan't forget it, not till my dying day.'

'You went down there!' Becky cried. 'Oh, Mum, *you* went!'

Else looked embarrassed, caught out.

'What else? Sat here till near midnight, waiting. Took me till then to think where he might have got to. And there he stood for all the world like a blessed statue. Would've stood there all night, if you ask me, till the dew got in his boots, if I hadn't thought to fetch him in.'

Finch did not contradict her. He had not even heard her. He was thinking, Becky realized between mouthfuls, with a thoroughness that was so complete that in all probability everything around him was blanked out, non-existent.

They all fell silent then. None, it seemed, was having the kind of thoughts that could be shared with the others. They thought privately, and painfully.

Breakfast over, Becky was sent back upstairs to wash, and brush her hair. That done, there was nothing to prevent her going out. She stepped through the back door and under the apple boughs, and the sun struck her with unaccustomed April heat. The cuckoo called, muffled, as if he were in a smother of leaves, bud breaking to leaf overnight now, covering his tracks.

Jason was waiting for her on a lean-to bench against a potting shed.

'Hello,' he said. 'Had a good spy, did you, last night?'

She nodded.

'*I* saw you, all right,' he said. 'Flitting about out here.'

'I went to bed after,' she told him. 'What happened?'

'*I* got sent off, as well. Not that it made any difference, the way that lot was shouting. You know what she's going to do, don't you?'

'Chop it,' said Becky.

'Chop, slash, chop, the whole lot of it. I'll tell you something. I wouldn't mind murdering Aunt Delia. Chop *her*.'

They stood there, helpless and hating.

'It's Sunday!' Becky cried suddenly. 'She can't!'

'Why can't she?'

'Under-gardeners' day off. All but a couple, anyhow. And they've got work to do. She can't make Dad do it single-handed. And he's got things to do as well. Biggest day for the public, Sunday is.'

'Well, all right,' he said. 'But tomorrow it'll be Monday!'

There was no argument at all about that. The Bongleweed was reprieved for a single day. All it really meant was that when the chop did come, it would be a bigger one.

They began to walk automatically towards the furthest corner of the work garden. The day was calm and green and beautifully April, a day between the showers. Becky could see the heads of the Bongleweed even over the tops of the glasshouses. The church tower was half green already and probably in bud.

As they approached, the sound of singing drifted towards them. It was singing beautifully clear and harmonious—the choir's set piece for the day. The inhabitants of Pew village were earnest, but not as a rule tuneful, in their rendering of hymns.

> *Morning has broken*
> *Like the first morning,*
> *Blackbird has spoken*
> *Like the first bird.*
> *Praise for the singing!*
> *Praise for the morning!*
> *Praise for them, springing*
> *Fresh from the Word!*

And it *is* like the first morning, Becky thought. Because it's all new. Adam and Eve, when they saw an apple tree, that was new, because it was the beginning of things. But the world's gone ordinary for us because we're used to it. It's gone usual.

She saw that the brave angel had gone and

wondered whether he was still blowing his trumpet down there under the green depths. The sun foamed on the sea of leaf and rearing flower and the music floated over it and it all swam into a blur.

Jason and me are Adam and Eve, she thought—or rather, did not think, but felt. And she dashed the tear from her eye and stared again at the Bongleweed with a kind of desperation, a fierce, futile attempt to make time stand still and the world stop new, for ever and ever.

There had been moments like this before. She recognized the feelings of joy and desperation inextricably mingled. 'You can put the fingers back on a clock, but you can't make *time* go back'—who had said that? Nor could you make time stand still. You might as well try to catch the wind in a net or trap light. The only way to keep things was by remembering, by calling things back out of the dust and breathing life into them again with love and passion.

Things could always be new, she thought, if we wanted them to be. It's us that're wrong. But I won't forget you, Bongleweed. Never, never never!

She said the words fiercely to herself and glared into the fugitive moment which even then was slipping away down the long corridors of the sunlight and already past capture.

Jason stood silent at her side and they must have stood for a long time because the organ began to peal loudly as the doors opened and the people came out. It was as if they stood on another shore, across the green sea, and they all stopped on the path and talked in groups and stared. They were so separate that even the sunlight between seemed thick and actual, a dividing mist of yellow.

Becky could not hear what they were saying and could only guess at their surprise. But it seemed to her even from that distance that they were nowhere near astonished enough. They could not have even half realized how strange a thing had happened in their midst, or even half seen how beautiful it was. They paused, looked, and in the end turned and walked on.

The organ stopped playing.

Next Sunday it'll be all gone, Becky thought. And perhaps they'll say 'Where's that pretty plant gone, that was here last week?' or perhaps 'I'm glad to see the parson's had the graveyard cleared at last'.

And she hated them all, for the Bongleweed's sake. It had done everything it could, thrown out its prodigal gifts of flower and greenery, burned itself out, for all she knew, to make things new again, to show them a first morning. But no one was looking.

Except us, she thought.

And for the Bongleweed that, surely, was cold comfort.

Chapter Fourteen

They wandered off in the end. It was not that they were bored, but because there was nothing you could *do* with the Bongleweed except stare at it, and be amazed all over again each time you saw it. It just *was*, and that was all there was to it.

'You know what,' said Jason suddenly. 'They might not be able to chop it.'

'Why not? There's about thirty of 'em, you know, counting the apprentices.'

'Yes, but listen. How magic *is* it? There's a story I heard once where they sowed dragon's teeth. And they came up as armed men, and when the people knocked one of them down, ten more sprang up in his place. Something like that. It might've been dragons that sprang up, not armed men.'

'More likely,' Becky agreed. 'With its being dragons' teeth for seeds.'

'But the point of it's the same, whichever it was!' He was excited now. 'What if the Bongleweed was like that? What if every time they chopped a stem, ten *others* sprang up in its place?'

They stopped now, and stared at one another in wild surmise.

'Think of it!' Becky cried. 'Ten times as big!'

'The church right under,' said Jason. 'Parson with it, with any luck!'

'And Pew—the whole village!'

'And then they'd have *another* chop!' he cried. 'Halfway to Brum, that'd take it!'

There rose again in Becky's mind the pictures she had seen the evening before of the village cocooned, the M1 in a silent green stranglehold.

'Could it? *Could* it?'

'We could always try it out,' said Jason thoughtfully. 'Do an experiment. We'd know then for sure.'

'I couldn't,' said Becky instantly. Nothing on earth would induce her to lay an axe into that innocent green. She doubted whether she could even bring herself to break off one of its flowers.

There was a pause.

'No,' said Jason at last. 'I couldn't, either.'

They walked on and found themselves passing through the arched gateway and into Pew itself. Becky, seeing it there calm and mirrored in the sunlight, felt the usual upsurge of love and admiration. Everything that grew here was planned and orderly—*meant*. But it was beautiful, and with a pang she knew that she did not *want* it to be swamped by a rampaging Bongleweed. What she wanted, she realized, was to have her cake and eat it.

And in any case, by the time they were halfway across the smoothly mown acreage of turf she found that she no longer believed in the story of the dragons' teeth. There were degrees of impossibility. The Bongleweed itself was impossible (if that was what you called a miracle). But it did have a kind of rhyme and reason, and was possible in the sense that it seemed to have a law of its own—a natural law. She did not for a moment believe in Jason's Mrs Crump in Brum, and nor did she believe in the dragons' teeth (or at least, she believed in them only insofar as they were truths unto *themselves*). For the Bongleweed, which had its own truth, to spring up again tenfold from the axe, would be *impossibly* impossible.

Her heart sank.

And tomorrow's Monday, she thought. Black Monday.

All she could do now in the time that was left was to stare and stare at the Bongleweed until it was so imprinted on her mind that she would never forget it, or cease to believe in it—not till her dying day, as Else herself had said.

'There's your father,' Jason said. 'Going to see Aunt Delia, by the look of it.'

She looked up. Finch was making steadily for the big house along a walk at the far side of the lawns. Next minute she was racing back the way she had come, back towards her own house, and the spyhole. The coast would be clear. Else would already have gone round to the big house—and in all likelihood would today be quashing her own scruples and herself be listening, from the kitchen, to the interview between Finch and Mrs Harper.

This morning, as she swiftly pushed aside the Bubble Boy, she had the fleeting illusion that his expression *had* changed, to one of sadness. But next minute her eye was at the spyhole just in time to see first Mrs Harper's slippers and, almost immediately in their wake, Finch's grey socks.

'Now, Finch,' began Mrs Harper almost at once, 'if you'd like to sit here . . . ?'

'Thank you, Mrs Harper, I'd rather stand,' Finch said. 'Thank you.'

As he spoke his face was in full view and Becky saw that there he would stay, stop rooted until the interview was at an end.

'Just as you like,' said Mrs Harper. 'I don't know what it is that you have to say to me, Finch, but there is certainly something I want to say to you.'

134

With a pang Becky saw how pale her father's face was. He seemed a different man—or rather, his old self, but changed, in some subtle way that she could not find words for.

'I daresay we both want to talk about the same thing,' he said then. 'But I should like to ask something. Have you heard from Doctor Harper yet? Or spoke to him?'

'Spoken to him?' cried Mrs Harper. 'In *Africa*?'

'No,' he said. 'That was what I thought.'

Becky saw him then draw in a deep breath, seem to stiffen, as if bracing himself to say something. He even opened his mouth—but too late.

'Yesterday,' said Mrs Harper, 'we had a

conversation about this peculiar weed. And I gave you some advice, as I remember.'

Nod.

'But apparently you did not take that advice. The Reverend Mr Waters was here last evening. As a matter of fact, I myself went to see the weed in question.'

Silence.

'I can only think that there were other matters more pressing,' she went on. 'And of course, this could well have been the case. But now, Finch, *nothing* is more pressing. I would like you, please, to take steps to exterminate this weed. Immediately.'

Silence.

'You understand me?'

Again Finch drew in the deep breath and his face, filling Becky's vision, seemed if possible whiter than ever.

'I must say now what I come to say, Mrs Harper,' he said. 'I never thought to ever say what I'm going to say. But I must. I want to hand in my notice.'

Silence. Not a Finch, but a *Harper* silence. Becky herself, astounded, stared one-eyed at her father's stiffened face and was filled with awe, horror, and jubilation in one overpowering rush of emotion.

'Oh, dear old Dad!' she cried silently. 'You *ain't*

going to chop it! But oh, Dad, what are you going and doing?'

'Notice?' came Mrs Harper's voice at last, on a high note. 'You wish to hand in your *notice*?'

'Yes,' said Finch. Even the one word was an effort now. He had braced himself up, said what he had come to say, and was finished now.

'But why ever should you do that? It's not to do with this ridiculous weed, I hope? I'm not *seriously* annoyed, Finch, and if you thought so, you have quite misunderstood me. There's no need at all for you to feel obliged to resign on that account. All I was going to say was that I'd like you to arrange for the weed to be destroyed at the earliest possible moment.'

Silence.

'In fact, I blame myself to some extent, for not going to see for myself what was taking place. You did your utmost to warn me, Finch, and I freely admit that I failed to realize the urgency of it all.'

Silence.

'So shall we leave it at that? You'll go along and make arrangements for the weed to be dealt with as soon as possible, and we'll say no more about the matter.'

Silence. Becky saw, or rather felt, her own anguish reflected now on Finch's face.

'Finch? Did you hear me?'

Another silence. A long one.

'I want to hand in my notice. I'm sorry.'

'But I don't *understand*!' she cried. 'Why should you wish to do such a thing? You, of all people! You're the doctor's right-hand man! You want to leave Pew, and go away?'

Finch shook his head.

'Leave Pew!' The enormity of what was happening struck Becky for the first time.

Mrs Harper, who did not know Finch at all, nor understand his code of nods and shakes, was near to desperation herself now.

'What do you mean?' she half wailed. 'Oh dear— all this, and the doctor heaven knows where . . . ! Now, Finch, you really must explain yourself.'

It was unbearable. Becky could not watch the dumb workings of her father's face an instant longer. She collapsed into the armchair. Then came Finch's voice.

'I can't chop that weed. I can't.'

'Can't? You mean—you don't want to get rid of it? You won't?'

'Can't. Won't. I'm sorry.'

'But, Finch, you've seen it for yourself! It's quite impossible—it's spreading on to Church property, and must be controlled. It isn't simply a matter of Pew. If you want to observe it—you say it's one of my husband's experiments—then surely you can keep just one small specimen? That would suffice—simply for the doctor to see on his return?'

Becky squeezed her eyes tight shut and waited for her father's reply.

'I should like to hand in my notice. I'm sorry.'

He could not explain. Perhaps he could hardly explain what he felt even to himself, let alone to Mrs Harper. Only one thing stood out perfectly clearly—Finch could not bring himself to kill the Bongleweed and would give up everything he loved rather than do so. And Becky could not bear to listen a moment longer, to hear Finch repeating again and again the only words he seemed able to say:

'I want to give in my notice. I'm sorry.'

She fled, leaving the deaf boy in the velvet suit to blow the stream of irridescent bubbles that would never burst because they floated out of time, because they were ever and ever bubbles, world without end. Becky could not hold conversation with him because he would not understand. For herself and the Bongleweed the clocks were ticking, the sun wheeling, the wind blowing, the world spinning and all things hastening to a certain end.

Chapter Fifteen

'He must do as he thinks right.'

It was the third time at least Else had spoken these words. The formula seemed to comfort her. Becky wondered whether her mother, faced with the choice, would have made the same decision. There was no real way of telling, but she rather suspected not. The Bongleweed had come into her life as an uninvited guest and had been made welcome. But to move house to make way for it was another matter entirely.

'But where'll we *go*, Mum?'

'We shall find somewhere. The world's a big place.'

That, Becky thought, was the whole trouble. The very word 'world' conjured up pictures of wild, windswept places, of tracklessness, wandering and homelessness. All the words that began with 'w' were daunting ones—wild, wet, wicked, weeping, want, and woe. World. It was something she could not come to terms with. She did not want to live in the world, she wanted to live in Pew.

She wished Finch would come and tell them what they were to do, where they were to go. But he had vanished. Dinner was ready and waiting to be served up and Finch was missing.

The very house was darkening. Becky did not like to go out of the kitchen because the passage was gone dim and green, its only light filtered through the dense leaves of the Bongleweed. What had been home was hardly home any more.

I wish I had an inkling, she thought.

She did not know exactly what an inkling was, but it seemed to fit the situation. It seemed to have something to do with seeing a flash or even a glimmer of light in the darkness of not knowing. Something to do with a swift splintering of a looking glass and then a remaking, so that when you looked again you saw a different reflection, one that made sense.

We need an inkling, she thought. There's no way out.

The situation seemed clear as crystal. The Bongleweed stayed and they went, or they stayed and the weed went. The alternatives were awful. She did not want to choose.

I want to have my cake and eat it, she thought, for the second time that day.

'Been ever so happy here,' she heard Else say. '*Never* did I think we'd leave.'

'Oh, Mum!'

The tears came then, and she clung to Else as she had not clung for years, smelling the polish and suds of her damp overall. She felt Else's hand awkwardly patting her head.

'There,' she said. 'There. Don't take on. Your dad'll find a way. Not the end of the world.'

The last words came on a gulp, followed by a sniff, and Becky did not raise her head because to see Else, of all people, in tears, would be more than she could bear. And as she clung the door opened and they sprang guiltily apart, each with a swift brush of the hand across the eyes. Else turned away to the stove.

'Dish up now, can I?' she said. 'Thought you was never coming.'

'I'm sorry, Else. Lost track of the time.'

Lost track of everything, Becky thought, and would have liked to fling her arms round him, too, but dared not. Finch was not looking for sympathy. He had done a brave thing after much thinking. He had done what he meant to do. He sat heavily in his chair.

'I'm sorry,' he said at length. 'I'm sorry, Else and Becky. Downright sorry.'

'Oh go on with you,' Else said. 'You get your dinner down you and stop worrying. Things'll sort 'emselves out.'

'You see,' he went on, 'it's as if something in me couldn't bring itself to do it. There's no sense in it, that I can see. No sense.'

'There's more'n sense to do with some things,' said Else surprisingly. 'Don't you go thinking *I* blame you. I don't.'

Finch got up then and went to the other door and stood for a minute gazing down the dim green passageway. From where she sat Becky could see the leaves through the little window above the front door.

'Dark now,' he said, and shut the door.

They sat round for dinner then, anchored to the familiar ritual in a safe place. But even as she ate Becky was aware that the wide world, the wild world was all around them, millions of miles of it, strange and hostile. Their house was a mere dot on a limitless map of space. She forced herself to swallow.

The minute she had finished she went out. Finch and Else were waiting to be alone, to say things they would never say in front of her.

Because they don't want me to be upset, she thought. And I *am* upset!

She went down towards the compost heap, because she wondered whether she could manage to hate the Bongleweed now. She wanted very much to hate it, so that her own life could be saved.

We were here first, she thought fiercely. Why should *we* go?

But when she saw the weed lying under the still heat of the April sun her heart leapt again as it always did when she saw it. It lay very quiet, as if it were holding its breath, but even in that windless calm Becky felt its life and strength. That and its beauty were undeniable. She could not hate it—still less could she wish it dead. The Bongleweed was a sign that all things were possible.

She even wondered—what if—?—what if the Bongleweed could draw in its horns, like a snail? Draw itself back into its seed again? But that was only another way of going back. For the Bongleweed, as for everything else in life, there was only one way to go—forward.

'Becky?'

Jason was behind her. She nodded.

'I'm sorry, Becky. I've heard. Aunt Delia's right off at the deep end. Says your father's out of his mind. And you know what she said?'

Finchlike, Becky shook her head.

'I said to her, "Look, Aunt Delia, Finch wouldn't hand in his notice just for nothing. Stands to sense he wouldn't. Why don't you go and have another look?" And you know what she said?'

Becky did not.

'She said, "Nothing would induce me to do

such a thing. Nothing!" And you know what I think? I think she's frightened. Scared stiff. It's how grown ups are, if things get beyond them. Try to pretend they're not there. And if they can't do that—chop 'em—like she's going to do with the Bongleweed. She's seen Porter already, you know.'

Porter was the head under-gardener, a big man with thick lips and a boxer's nose.

'Looks like an executioner,' went on Jason. 'Should've heard him sucking up, "Yes, Mrs Harper. No, Mrs Harper. Certainly, Mrs Harper." Thinks he's going to step straight into Finch's shoes.'

'He's got six children,' Becky heard herself say irrelevantly.

'Pity *them*,' he said. 'Thump, thump, thump from morning till night. And I bet he can pack a thump.'

'Oh, Jason, it's so sad! If you knew how my dad loves this place. And Mum. And me—*I* do! I don't want to go, I don't!'

They had sailed too long on calm waters and now they were shipwrecked.

'My father's moved jobs,' Jason said. 'Three times. But it's different, I suppose.'

'Oh, *your* father! What's that to do with it? My dad's different. My dad'll be coming up by his *roots*!'

Instead of the Bongleweed.

'I wonder . . .' mused Jason. 'I wonder whether . . . ?'

She did not prompt him.

'That witch in Brum,' he said. 'What if she could do something?'

'Oh shut *up* about her!' she whirled on him, ready to give her pent-up rage and sorrow an airing now. 'What's *she* to do with it, silly old woman! You keep your witches to yourself, will you. There ain't such *things*, I keep telling you!'

Silence.

'There aren't such things as Bongleweeds, either,' he said at last, and his voice was small and cold. 'Work *that* one out.'

And he went away. She heard his footsteps recede over the gravel.

Becky stood and gritted her teeth and cast round desperately for someone to blame. She blamed the doctor, for taking seeds, without question, from a bearded man who had obviously been the Devil—or one of his relations. She blamed her father for leaving the seeds carelessly lying there for Jason to pick up. She blamed Jason for sowing them, Mrs Harper, the vicar, the Stoneses, the—

She blamed herself. She looked at the Bongleweed and was looking at her own handiwork. And it was no use saying that she was sorry, even if she felt it (and even that was not certain). Her sorrow was so complicated and full of contradictions that she could not put it into words if even to herself. Some deep, unretractable part of her was not sorry.

Becky Finch, eavesdropper, spy, and sower of doom, was scared half out of her wits, filled with horrible guilt for what she had done to her family, but not, quite definitely not, sorry.

'You let rip, Bongleweed!' she whispered fiercely to the nearest foxes. 'You make hay, while the sun shines. Get growing, before that squashfaced Porter gets here. And come *this* way!'

She hesitated. Was it listening? Was she really giving an invitation?

'Come this way,' she repeated recklessly. 'You let the graveyard go and get *this* side of the fence!'

She had a glorious vision of Mrs Harper parcelled up in her tidy house and rushing hither and thither banging on windows to be let out.

And we wouldn't! she thought delightedly. Not even if we could! Let her do her own chopping for a change!

She stared grimly at the weed. Deny it she could not. So she did the opposite—she invoked it. She called upon it, silently, though with utter certainty that it understood, to do its worst—or best.

'Grow, Bongleweed, grow!' she commanded. '*Meant* to grow you are, so you do it, till you bust!'

She strained her eyes to see whether it was obeying or not—for the least sign of a thrusting stem or stretching tendril. And again she did not see, but *felt* its power, rising strongly as if drawing itself together for some tremendous effort.

Still she stood her ground.

'I ain't afraid, not me, whatever you do,' she said. 'So do it, Bongleweed! *Do* it! You hear me? You grow till you bust!'

Chapter Sixteen

The Bongleweed obeyed.

'Oh!' Becky gasped as the first green arm stretched out to take hold of a helping branch on her side of the railings. 'Oh sweet mystery of life! It's coming!'

The green arm took hold of the branch and held it with something very like a clenched fist.

'Now you stand fast, Becky Finch,' she ordered herself.

She stood very straight and looked ahead but from the corner of her eye was aware that a row, a whole long military row of green fists were fastening themselves to the railings. The Bongleweed, having marshalled its forces, was to advance now in order, it seemed, in ranks.

It's coming, all right! she thought. Now I *have* done it!

Before, she had only been half doing it. And now, stronger even than panic, came a rising sense of exultation, of release.

'Might as well be hanged for a sheep as a lamb!'

If the Finches were to be driven out into the wide, wicked, woeful, and weeping world, then they might as well make their reason a good one.

Give him something to sort out when he gets back this time, she thought, thinking of the doctor. Got a cross *here* he never reckoned on. Teach him, this will!

The Bongleweed came over the railings then, like a falling wave, with an audible slither of leaves.

'Teach us all!'

Becky held her ground.

The weed was whispering again now, blessing and hushing and guessing as it had that first night under the moon. And now, in broad daylight under the sun, Becky strained to hear what it was saying.

'Wish . . . loss . . . miss . . . ?'

She forgot to watch the weed, and listened instead. And what she caught was not a message or any kind of meaning at all, simply a string of tantalizing clues and half-meanings. She found herself half-hearing a word and, in wondering what it might be, sifting her own memories and being reminded of a thousand things she thought she had forgotten. She was like a drowning man who sees his whole life unreel before his eyes in the space of a few seconds.

It was not that she was in a dream. She knew that the sun was hot on her arms and could see the conspiratorial foxes hunting the weathercock and even thought how lucky it was for the cock that he was made out of brass, and inedible.

She could smell the smells that heat always draws out of the earth and from leaves—bitter-sweet like the scent of nettle and its flower both. She heard the cuckoo, too, but sounding strangely acceptable and real today, perhaps because she herself felt as mysterious as any cuckoo and so curiously light that it seemed perfectly possible that she had no shadow, either.

She looked to see and there it was, her shadow, shorter by half than herself and serrated at the edges because it lay on gravel.

Then her attention was distracted again by what the Bongleweed was saying, and it seemed to be saying 'face' and the face that rose before her mind's eye, instantly, was that of Porter, head under-gardener and executioner-to-be. She saw him minutely, the folds of flesh, the squat, flaring nose, and the brownish-red butcher's eyes.

As if he could do anything, she thought unconcernedly, so certain was she now that the Bongleweed was hers. She had made it, named it, and now at last suddenly knew that she could command it too.

She felt that every single bright fox was looking to her and for a moment was tempted to raise her arms and conduct them, like an orchestra.

'Becky! Becky!'

It was Else. Becky turned towards the house and saw that she was cut off. The Bongleweed had secretly and steadily encroached in a flanking movement, right across the work garden and as far as she could see. Else's face was a long way off and poking up among the foliage so scarlet that it might have been a fox's head itself.

'It's all right, Mum!' she shouted back.

'Finch! Finch!' Else's face was turned away now. 'Finch, come here, quick!'

Next minute there were two faces side by side. Those two familiar faces peered anxiously past the outsized leaves.

'Hello, Dad!' she shouted.

'Now you hold on, Becky,' called Finch. 'Hold on, there's a good girl, and I'll get you out!'

He disappeared.

'Dad!' she cried. Then, 'Where's he gone?'

'Now don't you panic, Becky,' came Else's voice. 'He's gone to fetch the axe. He'll get you out.'

'No! No!' At Becky's shriek Else's face went from red to white—a lone white fox in a green thicket.

'Becky, Becky love, we'll get you out!'

'You're not to! You're not to!' Becky stamped a foot invisible to Else but helping just the same. 'Let me alone! *I* can get out! I can!'

'Is there a way round the back?' cried Else. 'Behind?'

Becky looked behind and saw the Bongleweed there too. She was ringed by it—north, south, east, and westward. The only way out was skyward.

Oddly, the fact of her being at the centre of it made her all the more certain that she was its master. At arm's length she had been afraid. Now she felt herself very strong.

Finch's head popped up again and he lifted the axe reassuringly for her to see.

'No!' she shrieked. 'No! Let me alone! You're not to!'

'Becky love!' Else's voice came pleadingly over the intervening forest. 'You can't stop there for ever.'

'I can if I want!' Becky shouted back. 'And if you start chopping, I *shall*! I know how to get out by myself!'

The axe disappeared and she saw their two heads and faintly heard their voices in consultation. Back came Else's face.

'You tell us what you want us to do,' she said. 'Just tell us.'

'Go away. Go away. Please.'

She could see Finch's cap, and it was nodding.

'Dad!'

He must have stood on tiptoe then for her to see him.

'Go right away, Dad. Back to the house. I'm coming. But I want to be alone.'

The cap nodded.

Else's face reappeared.

'You hurry on up, then!' she cried, and next minute they had both gone.

Becky stood and waited for things (including herself) to settle again. Her heart was thudding hard and fast. Now that she had been offered safety and had turned it down, she felt the beginnings of terror. But she forced herself to look about her—wheeled round, pivoted on her shadow, fully recognizing that she was encircled.

It's me and a thousand foxes now, she thought. *Ten* thousand!

Then, out loud, she said, 'Bongleweed!'

It was the name she herself had given it, and a stir ran through the greenery at the sound of it.

'Bongleweed, let me by!'

She waited for only a few seconds and then began to walk deliberately towards the house as if the barrier did not even exist. Within a few paces she would be breasting the thicket but she went

155

steadily on and kept on, and on, and realized that what she had imagined would happen was actually happening.

The Bongleweed was falling away before her, parting as she advanced. She did not hurry, so certain was she of escape. She even had time to think, Like the Prince in the Sleeping Beauty. The weed fell back smoothly and with courtesy. She felt not so much as the brush of a leaf on arm or leg. She walked gladly between the green walls.

When she emerged and the walls were gone she felt queerly left in the lurch and exposed. What was left of the work garden seemed outsized and empty. She turned. The Bongleweed had closed, knitted itself together again.

'Good boy,' she said softly. If it had been a dog she would have patted it—given it a bone. But the Bongleweed, she knew very well, was not a dog—it was a fox, a tiger, a panther, a lion rampant. And she, Becky Finch, had tamed it. She stood a moment longer, and then:

'Whoopy whoop!' she yelled. 'Whoopy whoop!' and raced back home.

Chapter Seventeen

'You did *what*?' cried Else.

'Walked through.'

'Walked *through*?'

'Not exactly, Mum. It sort of opened up.'

'Opened *up*?'

Becky, tired of hearing her own words coming back to her like rudely emphatic echoes, turned to Finch instead.

'You see, Dad, there's no need to chop it! All I did was tell it to let me by, and it did.'

'Told it?' cried Else. 'As if it was to know? As if it had *ears*?'

'I *did* tell it out loud,' said Becky, 'but I needn't have. I could've told it inside my head. It knew.'

She saw Finch and Else exchange glances and saw that they did not believe her.

'It's true,' she said, though she really did not care whether they believed her or not.

Else got up.

'Come along then, Becky and Finch,' she said.

They rose and followed her. She marched ahead,

157

pinafore strings flying, back straight as a poker. A yard or two off the weed (and the weed had advanced another few feet since Becky had last seen it) she halted.

'Now, then,' she said.

No one spoke.

'Come along, then,' she said. 'Show us.'

'No!' Becky cried. She wished passionately now that she had not even told them.

'No, Mum! It's private.'

'Oh, *very* private,' said Else. 'Proper little shrinking violet, this is!'

Becky said nothing. Nor did Finch.

Else, thwarted, put her hands on her hips and surveyed the burgeoning Bongleweed.

'You try, then,' Becky said.

Else fell back a step.

'I shall do no such thing,' she snapped.

All three of them stood there, helpless as ever, as if Becky's escape was not a fact at all, had never happened. Becky herself felt suddenly annoyed with her mother for putting them into so awkward a situation, for not taking her story at face value.

'Go on, Mum,' she said. 'Not frightened, are you?'

Else's back went poker again. 'Such rubbish!'

She strode forward—three steps—and halted abruptly, just in time, a fox's head within an inch of her own nose. Becky laughed then—she could not help it.

'It don't bite!' she cried.

Else, very red in the face, whirled about.

'I daresay!' she cried. 'I daresay! But there's a limit, Becky, and this whole thing's gone too far!'

Becky, astonished by so swift a change of heart, stared.

'A weed's a weed,' went on Else, 'and as good as any other flower, I grant you that. And I'm not one for going pulling up innocent flowers left and right, as well you know, Becky and Finch. But it's all gone too far.'

'But it *hasn't*, Mum!' Becky cried. 'In fact, it hasn't gone far enough! It could cover the whole village, if it wanted to, the whole world!'

'It's gone too far,' repeated Else obstinately.

The silence was a long one.

'I'm coming to think we've done wrong,' went on Else herself at last. 'We've let the whole thing get out of hand.'

'You want to chop it?' cried Becky. 'You want Dad to chop it?'

Else looked uncomfortable.

'Well . . . *something*,' she said.

'Will you, Dad?' Becky turned to her father. He was not looking at them but at the Bongleweed, his head slowly shaking.

159

'You got to let nature take its course,' he said.

It was not a deep thought—in fact it was something Becky had often heard him say before, at one time or another. But today, at that particular moment in time, and confronted by a gigantic growth as *un*natural as anything Becky herself could imagine, it seemed deep. That simple statement seemed to tidy up the whole untidy matter. It seemed a solution, in the way that chopping or spraying or anything else had never seemed.

'Will it get a *chance*, though?' she said, thinking of Porter and his squad, probably sharpening their axes at this very moment.

'Not our worry, Becky,' Finch replied.

'And if it does—I mean Nature take its course— who's to say all England won't go under?' she persisted.

'Not our worry, Becky.'

Finch's needle had clearly stuck in a groove again, and so all the other questions Becky had in mind had to remain unasked.

'If you was to ask *me*,' said Else, 'I should say nature's nothing to do with it. That—' a jerk of her head towards the now disgraced Bongleweed— 'ain't nature.'

'Oh yes, Else. 'Tis,' said Finch. 'Anything that grows.'

'Like yeast in a bowl, I suppose,' said Else after a moment's thought, determined to catch him out.

'Aye. That too.'

'Never yet seen *yeast* with roots!' she cried, with what she supposed to be unanswerable logic, judging by the triumph of her expression.

'Didn't say with roots, Else. That grows. Changes. Moves on.'

'I can see it's no use my saying anything,' she said then. 'Set right against me, the pair of you. *And* that!'—another jerk of the head. 'But when I come to think, Finch, of the years we've had here, and the years we *was* to have, I could take an axe to that weed myself, for two pins!'

'Oh, Mum!' cried Becky. 'You couldn't!'

Else was saved from replying, or from having to prove herself, by a sharp dig in the ribs and a hiss from Becky.

'Look out! Porter!'

A broad-shouldered figure was framed in the arched gateway.

'Come on,' said Else, pulling at Finch's sleeve. 'Quick! Not stopping to be crowed over by him.'

Finch did not budge. In any case it was too late. Next minute Porter had arrived.

'Afternoon.' He managed to put a wealth of meaning into the word—menace, triumph, insolence

161

—things that had nothing whatever to do with the afternoon.

'Good afternoon,' replied Finch, unmoved.

'So that's it, is it?' remarked Porter. He put his hands on his hips and regarded the Bongleweed as if it was a mere bitty patch of groundsel.

Blind as a bat—must be! thought Becky, amazed that anyone on earth, even Porter, could see that soaring pack of radiant foxes for the first time and remain unmoved.

'Shouldn't take long to shift that lot,' he went on. 'No trouble there.'

Becky saw his tongue moistening his full red underlip, saw that he was actually relishing the task, and felt murderous.

'Got out o' hand, o' course,' he said. 'Missis says it's all over the graveyard, and all.'

The Finches remained silent. Porter, strong in the belief that Finch's boots would soon be empty and that he himself would step straight into them, was not ready to leave things at that.

'Given your notice, I hear, Finch,' he said.

'Given,' put in Else rapidly, before Finch could even open his mouth. 'Given, but not accepted. Twenty-four hours to make his mind up. Lot can happen in twenty-four hours, o' course.'

Porter smiled. It was an infuriating smile, and Else was duly infuriated.

'Pity some folk can't learn to mind their businesses,' she said. 'Pity some folk can't learn to let well alone.'

'Oh as to that, Mrs Finch,' said Porter pleasantly, 'we can't be doing with weeds like that. Not in Pew.'

'Don't you go lecturing *me* about weeds, Alfred Porter!' cried Else then. 'Finch knows more about weeds than you've got hairs on your head!'

The simile was an unfortunate one. Porter, as well as being ugly, was half bald. Both face and bald patch reddened visibly.

'What this has got to do with ain't nothing to do with what's weeds and what isn't,' he said. 'It's to do with carrying out instructions given. By your employer.'

'Lucky for you your employer ain't here, then!' snapped Else. 'Doctor Harper's your employer, so far as I know, and not giving instructions from China or Timbuktoo or wherever he is, *I* know!'

'Now, Else,' began Finch. But he had left it too late. Else was in full spate now.

'*That*,' she cried, stabbing a finger towards the Bongleweed, 'is *nature*, Alfred Porter! And so far as I know, there's only one thing to be done about nature, and that's to let it take its course!'

Becky gasped.

'That!' Porter was shouting now. 'That's no more nature than I am!'

'And *that's* true!' returned Else. 'Nothing natural about you, Alfred Porter. Chop, chop, chop—all you can think about, that is. Butcher you should've been, let alone gardener. And I'll tell you something else. I could chop my yeast when I was baking, I could chop chop chop it till I was blue in the face and it'd still rise, because it's nature, that is! So what do you say to that?'

Porter, evidently dazed by the rapid twists and turns the argument was taking, could say nothing to

that. Else, taking advantage of his confusion, pressed on.

'If I was you,' she said, 'I should be careful of what I said. *Ever* so careful. You're in front of witnesses!'

She waved an arm that seemed to include the Bongleweed and its foxes as well as the Finches themselves.

'And there's many a slip 'twixt cup and twenty-four hours, you remember that!'

A gesture with the other arm seemed to indicate the boundlessness of those possibilities, and even gave Else, both arms now upraised, the momentary look of a prophetess of doom about to call down a flock of vultures or heaven knows what other calamities.

This was how it must have seemed to Porter, because he took advantage of the lull to nod hastily towards Finch, servile once more, and beat a retreat towards Pew.

'Tail between his legs!' as Else described it later, going over the scene in detail at supper-time—with some danger to the crockery in the enaction of certain parts. 'Tail between his legs like a squashed caterpillar! We'll see who laughs last!'

'But I did hand in my notice, Else,' Finch reminded her. 'And if I am to go, odds are he *will* get my job. Temporary, anyhow.'

'Don't you forget,' Else wagged a finger. 'There's many a slip!'

There was a silence while they thought about this.

'Though I can't think what,' she admitted at last, and the finger fell.

'Well, we shall have to see,' Finch said. He got up. 'Work's to be done. Right chilly now the sun's dropped—I shall have to see to my frames. Time for a frost or two yet.'

He went out.

'Just like your father, that is,' said Else, with a sigh that was half proud, half regretful. 'Him all over. A time like this, and worrying over frames. I can see that Porter getting up from his supper to see to frames. If your father goes, this place'll be to rack and ruin in a twelvemonth. If Doctor Harper wasn't gallivanting off in China there's none of this'd ever've happened.'

'Africa, Mum.'

'*He* knows who it is keeps Pew going,' Else went on. 'I'll give him that. "I don't know what Pew would do without you, Finch!"—the times I've heard him say that . . .'

Becky saw that Else was about to embark on a long string of reminiscences.

'I think I'll get off to bed, Mum,' she said. 'I'm tired.'

'Bless your heart, I should think so!' cried Else at once, with such warmth that Becky felt ashamed. 'All these goings on! You get off to bed, and don't you worry your head about a single thing. Your father and me'll sort things out, never fear.'

You won't, Becky thought as she climbed the stairs. She had to turn on the light to see her way. It was dusk outside, but black as night in the hall and passageway. 'It's the Bongleweed'll sort things out, now.'

She switched on the light in her room and saw the foxes at the window folded now into moths for the night.

No need to draw the curtains, really, she thought. And then she shivered, suddenly cold— or afraid—or both. She drew the curtains.

She lay awake for a long time after she had turned out the light, as she had meant to do. She thought about the Bongleweed, and every now and again a moth or a leaf brushed lightly against the glass close by. She was still half awake when Else came up to pull the blankets tight and bless her.

Then she fell asleep.

Chapter Eighteen

Becky slept uneasily. She had dreams full of foxes and butchers and spent long hours wandering alone through strange landscapes—the wild world.

She awoke abruptly from one of these dreams. The first sensation she had was one of cold. Half opening her eyes she saw that her eiderdown had slipped on to the floor, no doubt during one of her flights from an axe-bearing butcher. She sat up and shivered.

'Tis cold, she thought, and realized at the same time that it was dawn. The curtains were faintly lit from behind and she could hear birds twittering. She pulled the eiderdown up again and lay back, prepared to go back to sleep. But she could not. Something was nagging at the back of her mind. Drowsy as she was, she was aware of a paradox, of something that did not fit.

'The light!' she cried, and sat up again. 'That's it!'

If it was only just dawn, why was the room

faintly lit, when by rights it should be darkened still by the Bongleweed? She ran to the window and pulled back the curtain.

'Oh!' Between a gasp and a wail. 'Oh! Oh no!'

Winter had come again in the night, silent as frostfall. The ground was white down below and looking up she could see in the distance the white curve of the hillside against the thin grey sky.

Frost had struck and the Bongleweed was burned out, blackened as if by fire. It had shrunk, shrivelled to a ghost of its former self. Its black framework was stark against the frost and leaning already for the final fall. Of the moth-foxes there was not a sign. The Bongleweed had gone, as it had come, in the night.

Becky, her teeth chattering violently, stared desperately down under the sill for the least sign of survival, for a single green shoot that might spring to life again when the April sun came out.

'Oh it's gone!' she shivered, and then, 'Mum! Dad!'

She ran out and along the passage and into their room. Else and Finch lay peacefully asleep, Finch snoring gently (Not a bit like a grampus! she thought fleetingly).

'Mum! Dad!'

Else shot up, blinking rapidly.

'What? What?'

'Mum—the Bongleweed! Wake Dad!'

But Finch was already awakening, slowly but surely as he did everything else, and thoroughly. When he opened his eyes he looked straight at Becky and said:

'Why, Becky, what's to do, lass? It's night yet.'

'T'ain't, Dad, it's dawn! And it's frosted in the night and oh, Dad, the Bongleweed!'

He had his legs over the side of the bed now and his feet were groping for his slippers.

'Come on, Mum!'

Else had her dressing-gown on and began to pad after Becky along the passage, pulling out her curlers automatically as she went and slipping them into her pocket.

'Ooooh!'

One look through the window and she let out a shriek that fetched Finch, despairing of his second slipper, limping fast to join them.

The doves were out now in cautious exploration, crossing flights between the black forks and spires, then returning to safe perches to coo out their bewilderment, work it all out. In the bleak dawn light the scene was one of desolation, the end of the world.

'So that was it!' said Else at last.

The others went on staring.

'The slip,' she explained, as much to herself as anyone else. ' 'Twixt cup and today.'

No colour in the morning at all. White, grey, black. A sketch of the world.

'Nature too, Else,' Finch said then. 'Taking its course.'

'But it's cruel!' Becky cried. 'It's not fair! That beautiful Bongleweed and all them foxy heads it grew, all huge and orange and—oh and look at 'em now!'

The sight of the black tangle that had once been a rare green glory such as no English April had ever bred before was too much for her. She threw herself on the bed and sobbed bitterly.

There was no trace of relief in her tears, no relief that the Finches were safe now, need not set forth into a cold world. Her tears were all of grief, pure grief, for the death of the Bongleweed. Dead, all that wild and wonderful green, dead the bright foxes that had folded to moths at twilight, dead the only miracle she might ever see.

'There, now.' She felt Else's hand on her shoulder. 'Don't take on, now.'

But Becky did take on. She could not help herself.

'Oh dear, oh dear,' she heard her mother say. 'I'll go down and put the kettle on.'

Becky went on sobbing. There was no comfort.

No one else had made, known, and loved the Bongleweed as she had, and so no one could comfort her. She felt the eiderdown being placed over her, then heard Finch's one slippered foot going away.

When at last she had cried herself out she got up and went to the window again. The sun had come up while she was not looking and already only the shadows were left white and were being eaten away minute by minute. The frost was melting. It was going to be a beautiful day.

There's one thing . . . she thought. I can always see it again, if I want . . .

Already she could, in her mind's eye. She saw every detail. The gay foxes leapt into flower and nodded bright as ever and the graveyard went fathoms deep under green again. Becky, eyes shut tight, found herself actually smiling.

'Whenever I want . . .' she murmured. 'And there's another thing . . .'

In a world where once a Bongleweed has sprung, anything would be possible, from now on. Perhaps *another* Bongleweed, clinging tenaciously to life down among the frosted roots, ready to wax again in the warmth and showers of April. Or perhaps it would be something quite different— out of the blue—desperate, beautiful, reckless— *anything*!

She opened her eyes and glared fiercely down at the innocent, melting garden where the white was almost visibly yielding now to the green.

You wait! she thought exultantly. Just you wait!

Becky opened the window and felt her skin shrivel. She leaned right out above the blackened branches of the Bongleweed and drew in the heady smell of frost and was at once certain, in her very bones, that the world itself was both alert and mysterious as those foxes' heads had been. The world had gone once and forever wild on her very doorstep.

'Becky!'

There was Jason, in his dressing gown and slippers in the drive below.

'Becky! It's dead!' His face was white and thinned by shock.

She felt herself a long way off from him, separated not only by distance but by a grief that was already changing into a promise.

'Not dead,' she heard herself say.

'But it is! I've been round the other side—it's dead, all of it! Oh damn the frost, damn it!'

'It's nature,' she said, 'I s'pose. Taking its course.'

'Nature!' His voice went high and sharp. 'It was *magic*—you said so yourself. You know it was. What's the matter with you. Aren't you *sorry*?'

Becky shivered.

'Oh, idiot!' she cried, furious to find her eyes filled again. 'What do you think? But there'll be another, don't you see? There'll be another!'

Silence. He stared blankly up at her.

'Another what?'

'Oooh!' She let out a cry of exasperation at what seemed like a deliberate blindness.

'I haven't decided yet!' she told him, and banged the window.

She dressed then, and went slowly downstairs.

'Here you are.' Else handed her a cup of tea. 'We was all fond of that weed, Becky, in our own ways.'

'A cross, you see, Becky,' said Finch, 'and must've had a touch of tropical in it. Too hot in glasshouse, too cold outdoors—not easy to raise, you see.'

'No, Dad.' She did not really want to talk about it.

'Had a good run for its money, though,' offered Else. 'Didn't it just! Showed that Porter a thing or two!'

Showed us all a thing or two, Becky thought.

'I should like to see his face this morning,' went on Else, who never took very long to see the bright side of anything. 'Put a right blight over his morning, this will.'

She started to bang pans, warming to her theme.

'And all them axes sharpened. Axes sharpened and nothing to chop. You set him on clearing up what's left, Finch, all them blacked-up branches. Nice back-breaking job for somebody, that'll be. Hand in *his* notice, I shouldn't wonder!'

'Better be getting along,' said Finch, and rose from the table. 'Coming, Becky?'

She nodded.

'And you get your coat on,' ordered Else. 'It'll be cold yet.'

Becky and Finch stepped out together into the still-white shadow of the house and the pocket of cold that seemed to have collected under the boughs of the apple. A few steps and they were in the sun. When they reached the arched gateway Becky looked back. Half-blinded by the sun still, she could see the church tower streaked black.

Then she followed her father into Pew, on to the wet, white, and dazzling lawns, taking her first difficult steps into a world without the Bongleweed. But now it was a world where the Bongleweed had been, and that would make all the difference.

Other Oxford books

The Piemakers
Helen Cresswell
ISBN 0 19 271809 6

Arthy, Jem, and Gravella Roller are the finest pie-makers in Danby Dale, famed for their perfect pastry and fantastic fillings. So when they're asked to make a special pie for the king, which will feed two hundred people, the Rollers are thrown into a frenzy of excited preparations. This will be the best ever Danby Dale pie! But unfortunately, wicked Uncle Crispin, a rival pie-maker, has different plans for the Rollers' pie . . . plans that include an extra-large helping of pepper . . .

This funny, charming story was Helen Cresswell's first children's book, and was nominated for the Carnegie Medal

How to Survive Summer Camp
Jacqueline Wilson
ISBN 0 19 275019 4

Typical! Mum and Uncle Bill have gone off on a swanky honeymoon, while Stella's been dumped at Evergreen Summer Camp. Guess what? She's not happy about it!

Things get worse. Stella loses all her hair (by accident!), has to share a dorm with snobby Karen and Louise, and is forced into terrifying swimming lessons with Uncle Pong! It looks as if she's in for a nightmare summer—how can Stella possibly survive?

Temmi and the Flying Bears
Stephen Elboz
ISBN 0 19 275015 1

Temmi is furious when the Witch-Queen's soldiers come to the village to steal one of the flying bears—even more so when he discovers that they've taken Cush, the youngest cub, who is Temmi's favourite bear. Temmi is determined to rescue Cush, but instead finds himself captured and taken to the Ice Castle where he will be a prisoner, too. Escape seems impossible—unless Temmi can somehow win over the ice-hearted Queen . . .

'Stephen Elboz is an exciting new literary talent'

The Independent

Atlantis
Frances Mary Hendry
ISBN 0 19 275017 8

Far below the Antarctic ice, the folk of Atlantis have lived in safety for
centuries. But when a boy called Mungith makes an unbelievable
discovery in the old mines, the Atlantans' lives are suddenly in great
danger. Then tragedy hits the kingdom, and Mungith knows he will
be blamed—unless he can somehow restore peace and wellbeing to his
people . . .

Atlantis in Peril
Frances Mary Hendry
ISBN 0 19 275018 6

The peaceful kingdom of Atlantis is once again in great danger.
Chooker realizes that the only way to restore the good name of her
family and protect the kingdom is to make the journey to Outside.
And when the King's wicked sister tries to kill her, it only makes
Chooker realize how urgent her mission is . . .

Starlight City
Sue Welford
ISBN 0 19 275041 0

It is the year 2050. When Kari's mother brings home Rachel, a strange
woman she finds wandering in the street, Kari is horrified. What does
her mother think she's doing, picking up a scruffy old Misfit—or even
a Drifter?

But far from being a con-woman, Kari finds Rachel gentle and
intelligent—and in trouble with the law. So when the police arrive and
take her away, Kari decides she must go to the City and look for
Rachel, embarking on an adventure that will change both of their lives
for ever . . .

Outcast
Rosemary Sutcliff
ISBN 0 19 275040 2

Sole survivor of a shipwreck as a baby, Beric is an outsider from the start. The village druid warns that he is cursed by the sea, and when death comes to the tribe, the fingers of blame point in only one direction.

Cast out by the warriors, Beric is left alone without friends or family. With no home and little money, he must survive in harsh Roman Britain by himself, with death, danger and enemies always around the corner . . .

Outcast is one of an exciting series of novels about Roman Britain, by the award-winning author Rosemary Sutcliff.

Oxford Fairy Tales

Fairy Tales from England
James Reeves
ISBN 0 19 275014 3

Giant-killing Johnny Gloke, a princess with a sheep's head, and a frog prince at the World's End are just some of the fairy-tale characters you'll find in this collection of stories, along with better-known tales such as Dick Whittington and Tom Thumb. Greedy giants, handsome princes, wicked queens, and a liberal sprinkling of magic all help to make sure this collection of traditional English fairy tales has something for all the family.

Fairy Tales from Scotland
Barbara Ker Wilson
ISBN 0 19 275012 7

Gallant knights, the enchanting Elf Queen, witches, wizards, and wee faery folk . . . you'll find them all in this exciting collection of Scottish fairy tales and legends. Whether you prefer Highland legends, ancient sagas, or warrior adventures, there's something for everyone in this collection—along with a good helping of Gaelic magic!

Fairy Tales from Grimm
Peter Carter
ISBN 0 19 275011 9

Cinderella, Snow White, Sleeping Beauty, Rumpelstiltzskin . . . everyone knows and loves the famous fairy tales of the Brothers Grimm. In this collection, award-winning novelist Peter Carter has translated from the original German texts to bring you a feast of favourite tales in one volume. Read on for wicked witches, beautiful princesses, greedy wolves and more, all told with vivid imagery and wit.

Fairy Tales from Andersen
L. W. Kingsland
ISBN 0 19 275010 0

The Ugly Duckling, Thumbelina, the Snow Queen and the Little Mermaid are just some of the magical characters in Hans Christian Andersen's famous fairy tales. This collection has all the well-loved favourites, as well as some of Andersen's lesser known stories, and is bound to enchant new readers as much as it will please those who are already familiar with these classic stories.

One Thousand and One Arabian Nights
Geraldine McCaughrean
ISBN 0 19 275013 5

'Woman's love is as long as the hairs on a chicken's egg!'

So says King Shahryar who kills a new wife every night, before she can stop loving him. But new bride Shahrazad has a clever plan to save herself. Her nightly stories—of Sinbad the Sailor, Ali Baba, and the Jinni of the Lamp—are so exciting that King Shahryar finds himself postponing her execution again and again . . .

This is a completely original version of the Arabian Nights by award-winning author Geraldine McCaughrean.

'A brilliant tour de force'

Junior Bookshelf